After Emily ha e and left, Jillian sna— — face. "Earth to Dr. —

He jumped. "Oh, so—

She smiled as she shook her head and sat back down at her desk. "You've got it bad."

"Huh?"

"You really like that girl, don't you?"

Noah blinked and turned to face her. "Yes, she seems very nice. Why?"

"She's more than nice. I saw how the two of you looked at each other." Jillian held up a stack of paperwork she hadn't yet filed. "You were right about needing some help around here. I sure hope she decides to take you up on your job offer."

"Yeah, me, too."

As Noah headed back to tend to one of the animals, he heard her mumble. It sounded strangely like, "Yeah, I bet you do."

DEBBY MAYNE has been a freelance writer all her adult life, starting with slice-of-life stories in small newspapers and then moving on to parenting articles for regional publications and fiction stories for women and girls. She has been involved in all aspects of publishing, from the creative side to editing a national health magazine to freelance proofreading for several book publishers. Her belief that all blessings come from the Lord has given her great comfort during trying times and gratitude for when she is rewarded for her efforts. She lives on the west coast of Florida with her husband and two daughters.

Books by Debby Mayne

HEARTSONG PRESENTS
HP625—Love's Image
HP761—Double Blessing
HP785—If the Dress Fits

Noah's Ark

Debby Mayne

Heartsong Presents

Thanks to Kathleen Lamb who works with her husband, Dr. Scott Lamb, at the Trinity Animal Hospital in New Port Richey, Florida, for answering my animal questions.

I'd like to thank Brenda Holley, Member Relations coordinator with the Huntington, West Virginia, Chamber of Commerce, for providing information specific to the area.

Also, thanks to Byron Clercx, chairman of the Department of Art and Design at Marshall University, Huntington.

A note from the Author:
I love to hear from my readers! You may correspond with me by writing:

Debby Mayne
Author Relations
PO Box 721
Uhrichsville, OH 44683

ISBN 978-1-60260-592-3

NOAH'S ARK

Our mission is to publish and distribute inspirational products offering exceptional value and biblical encouragement to the masses.

PRINTED IN THE U.S.A.

one

Emily Kimball opened the sunroof on her nearly ten-year-old Nissan as she hummed to a country tune on the radio. Free from the constraints of a schedule, she felt a slight sense of freedom—something she'd never experienced in her life. After quitting her job at an art supply company and selling everything she didn't absolutely need, there was nothing left to hold her back.

Sunlight flickered as the sugar maples and oaks thickened on either side of the West Virginia country road. The hills provided a wall of foliage in varying shades of green. Although Emily had never lived in Huntington, she'd visited enough for the familiarity of it to feel like home.

The old farmhouse came into view, giving her a fluttery sensation in her chest. She blinked but not in time to hold back a tear that slipped down her cheek. Last time she'd been here had been a celebration—a family reunion. Her aunt and uncle had a way of making her forget her mother was no longer around. This visit was different. She needed to figure out what she wanted out of life, and she needed the strength of someone who loved her nearby.

Aunt Sherry sat on the swing that Uncle Mel had suspended from the front porch ceiling when Emily was a little girl—back when her parents were still together and her father was still alive. She remembered the sensation of floating as she and one of the adults in her life swayed to the rhythm of the night birds chirping. Back then, she had no idea her mother would decide she wasn't cut out for family life and abandon her and her father as soon as Emily hit puberty.

Her aunt glanced up right before Emily turned onto the

narrow paved driveway leading to the house. Emily turned off the radio, slowed down as she approached, and stopped in the exact same spot where her parents always parked whenever they came to West Virginia to visit.

"Mel!" Aunt Sherry hollered. "Emily's here!"

"Be right out!" Uncle Mel's husky voice flooded Emily with even more nostalgia.

Aunt Sherry didn't waste another second before heading straight to the driver's side. As soon as Emily opened the door and stood up, Aunt Sherry pulled her into an embrace that smelled of apple dumplings and cinnamon.

"I can't believe you're really here." Her aunt held her at arm's length and looked her over, smiling the entire time. "It's been years since we've seen you."

Emily cast a glance down at the ground, embarrassed that she'd let so much time lapse since her last visit. "I—uh, I missed you."

Aunt Sherry flipped her hand from the wrist. "Don't you worry about it. You're here now, and that's all that matters." She gave Emily another hug. "Come on in, sugar. I've been cooking up a storm, ever since I heard you were coming." She put her arm around Emily's waist and guided her toward the house. "I bet you're starving."

"I am a little hungry."

"Well, I'll be. . ."

Emily glanced up and saw Uncle Mel coming out of the house, arms open wide. "Uncle Mel!"

Ignoring the steps, he hopped down off the side of the porch and strode toward her. "You sure have grown up, young lady. In fact, you look just like your mama when she was your age."

Aunt Sherry shot him a warning glance. "Mel, this isn't the time."

He snorted and winked at Emily before turning to his wife. "It's not a secret that her mama was a looker, and there's definitely no hiding that our little Emily is just as pretty."

He focused his attention back on Emily. "You look just like a movie star. All the boys in church will be gawking at you."

Emily's cheeks heated with embarrassment, and she allowed her aunt to take control. "Mel, the poor girl has just arrived. Where are your manners? At least show some hospitality and give her time to rest before you start in on her."

"I'm just sayin'. . ."

"Emily, sugar, why don't you give your uncle your car keys, and he can bring your things in?"

As soon as Emily handed her uncle the keys, he left the two women alone. Aunt Sherry led her the rest of the way to the kitchen, which Emily could have found with her eyes closed. All she had to do was follow the aroma that grew stronger with each step.

"Have a seat, sugar, and I'll cut you a slice of pie. We have apple, custard, and chocolate. Which one do you want to start with?"

Emily laughed. "You're still determined to make me fat, aren't you?"

"You never did have much of an appetite. It's no wonder you've always had a hard time keeping meat on those bones." She pulled a knife from the kitchen drawer and turned to face Emily. "Is custard still your favorite?"

"I think I'd like chocolate today."

Aunt Sherry chuckled. "Chocolate's always been my favorite. That's what I'll have, too." She cut each of them a generous slice and added a dollop of whipped cream before setting the plates on the table and lowering herself into the chair adjacent to Emily. "I'm glad you're here. It's been getting mighty lonely, with just Mel and me."

"I don't know how to thank you for letting me stay here until I figure out what I want to do with my life." Emily cut the tip of the pie and raised it to her mouth to savor the taste. "This is delicious."

Aunt Sherry took a bite and nodded. "It was your grandma's

recipe. While you're here, I'll teach you how to make it."

Emily didn't plan to be there long enough, but since she didn't want to rattle any cages, she just smiled and cut another bite of pie.

"Tell me all about what you've been up to since you graduated from college." Aunt Sherry paused for a moment, her fork suspended over her pie. "Last I heard before your call was you had a great job. What happened?"

Emily crinkled her face and scrunched her nose. "The job wasn't what I thought. I wanted to do customer service, and they had me making sales, complete with quotas."

Her aunt offered a sympathetic look. "Isn't that the way it goes sometimes? Why, those people ought to be ashamed of themselves for telling you one thing then doing another."

"I'm afraid I'll have to take some of the blame. I was so desperate for a job I didn't pay much attention to the full job description until I accepted the position. When I realized what I was about to do, I tried to make the most of it." She paused as she traced her fork over what was left of her pie, then she looked her aunt in the eye. "But with all the things happening in my life, I couldn't focus on something I didn't have my heart in, especially after a new manager came in and acted like I didn't have a brain in my head. That only lasted a few weeks. I just wish I knew what I wanted to do."

"If it's any consolation, sugar, I didn't have any idea what I wanted when I was your age. Mel and I had been married a year, so I stayed in my dead-end job because I didn't know what else to do."

"Then we had kids." The sound of Uncle Mel's voice by the kitchen door instantly caught their attention. "It's amazing how babies can change your life." He chuckled. "Then they grow up, and you find yourself wondering what happened."

Emily smiled. "I'd like to have children someday but not until I figure out who I am first."

"And you need to meet the right man," Aunt Sherry

reminded her. "A man who loves the Lord as much as you do."

"Absolutely." Emily wasn't even sure if such a man existed, at least one who would love her for who she was—a very confused daughter of a mother who took off at the first sign of teenage angst.

Aunt Sherry gestured to one of the empty chairs. "Have a seat, Mel, and I'll cut you a piece of pie."

"Maybe later. I'm waiting for the chickens. Noah should be here any minute."

Emily turned to her uncle. "Chickens? Who's Noah?"

"Noah's the vet we brought in a little more than a year ago. We renamed the old animal clinic *Noah's Ark*."

"With a name like Noah, what else could you have done?" Emily asked with a grin.

Her aunt and uncle both laughed, and then Uncle Mel turned serious. "Anyway, after that last flood in the valley, a bunch of livestock had to be rescued. Noah and some of the other fellas got there just in time."

"So. . .the chickens were rescued from the farms?" Emily was still confused.

"Yep. And Noah's bringing a whole bunch of 'em here."

Aunt Sherry made a clicking sound with her tongue. "We haven't had chickens in quite a while. It'll take some getting used to, having them around here again."

"Better get used to it, Sherry," Mel said. "Noah can't handle all the animals without a little help from friends."

"And the Lord," Aunt Sherry added.

Mel cupped his ear with his hand. "I think I hear the truck comin' now. Y'all wanna go help?" He took a quick glance at Emily. "You might wanna change out of those nice clothes. Chickens can get you pretty dirty."

"What are you trying to do to our guest, Mel? She just got here. Give her a chance to relax."

Emily stood and carried her plate over to the sink. "I don't mind helping. I'll be right out."

Uncle Mel had already gone outside, but Aunt Sherry paused by the door, a look of consternation on her weathered face. "You really don't have to, but I'm not one to turn down an offer of help."

"Just let me find my jeans, and I'll join you all in a few minutes."

Aunt Sherry took off outside to help Uncle Mel, leaving Emily alone in the old farmhouse. Nothing had changed much. The wood-paneled walls provided warmth and welcome. The only rooms not lined with wood were the bedrooms and bathrooms, all painted in soft pastel colors to add a hint of cheer. Emily walked down the wide hallway with the locked gun closet on one side and bedrooms on the other. She peeked in every room looking for her things. When she got to the end of the hallway, she smiled. Emily was delighted that Uncle Mel had put her bags in the creamy yellow bedroom, her favorite.

She walked around the trunk filled with memorabilia, opened the bigger of the two suitcases, and found jeans and a T-shirt. As soon as she changed, she pulled her hair up into a ponytail and headed outside to lend a hand.

Uncle Mel stood beside an old pickup, taking crates from a dark-haired man bent over in the bed of the truck. He grinned and motioned for her to join them.

"Where's Aunt Sherry?"

The squawking chickens drowned out Uncle Mel's answer as he bent over and picked up another crate.

☙

At the sound of a different voice, Noah straightened and found himself looking at the prettiest woman he'd seen since he'd been in West Virginia. Her eyes widened as they stared at each other.

"Noah Blake, meet my niece, Emily Kimball." Mel turned and faced Emily. "Noah's the veterinarian we told you about earlier."

Just as Noah was about to jump off the back of the truck to shake Emily's hand, Sherry came out of the barn. "I thought I heard Emily out here. Why don't you come help me get these chickens situated?"

Noah turned to see Emily shade her eyes with her hand. "I'll be right there, Aunt Sherry." Then she swung back around and faced him with her cornflower-blue eyes focused directly on him. "Nice to meet you, Dr. Blake."

He smiled back at her. "Just call me Noah."

She blinked. "Okay, Noah." Then she took off and disappeared into the barn before he had a chance to say another word.

Mel belted out a chuckle. "Her mama had that kind of impact on men. Too bad she wasn't half the woman Emily is."

"Huh?" Noah was dumbstruck, first by his own reaction to Mel and Sherry's niece then by Mel's comment.

"Emily is a sweet Christian girl—takes after her daddy. Her mama never stepped foot inside a church after the wedding. It's no wonder she didn't stick around when the goin' got tough."

Noah still hadn't gotten used to the openness of these West Virginia folks. He'd just learned more about Emily Kimball than he knew about his housemates from college.

"How many more loads of chickens you got?" Mel asked.

"Um. . .let's see." Noah forced his thoughts back on the task at hand. "Two more?"

Mel lifted his eyebrows and let out a snort. "I reckon you better head out and get 'em before it gets dark. Suppertime will be here before you know it."

"I don't have to bring all of them here," Noah said. "Clayton said he could make room in his barn."

"Nah, better not do that. He has enough of his own cacklers to deal with. No sense in getting them all mixed up."

Noah hoisted the last crate from the truck, handed it off to Mel, and brushed his hands together. "I wasn't sure if you had time for this, with your niece being here and all. I figure you don't want to miss a minute of precious time you can spend with her." What he wanted to know was how long pretty Emily with the gorgeous blue eyes and wavy, honey-colored hair would be staying, but he didn't want to come right out and ask.

Mel's eyes squinted as he cast a long look at Noah. "That girl's been around barnyard animals before. I reckon she doesn't mind."

"She likes animals?"

"Yes, of course she likes animals," Mel said. "She's related to me, isn't she?"

Noah laughed. "She's been living in the city, so I wasn't sure."

Mel planted his fists on his hips and looked him squarely in the eye. "How would you know she's been living in the city?"

Busted. Noah glanced down then back up at Mel. "Sherry told me."

"I figured as much." Mel motioned for Noah to join him.

They finished unloading the truck and getting the chickens situated in half the time Noah expected. "I don't know how to thank you, Mel."

Mel made a face. "You don't have to keep thanking me for what I offered to do. C'mon, let's help the ladies and get the rest of these chickens in the barn so we can be done before dark. You're stayin' for supper."

"I can't—"

"Nonsense. It's the least we can do."

Noah appreciated the values of these rural West Virginia people—how they did favors yet considered it a privilege and insisted on paying people for allowing them to do favors by feeding them. This was something he wasn't used to.

A half hour later, Noah was on his way to pick up the next batch of chickens. A year ago he never would have pictured himself working at the outskirts of Huntington, West Virginia, with his clients' livestock on family-owned farms. When he first got into vet school, he assumed he'd take over for his father, who had a small-animal practice in a ritzy area of Atlanta. However, when he heard about the need for someone in West Virginia, he decided to check it out. The moment he crossed the line into some of the most beautiful, mountainous countryside, he knew he'd come home.

The people were amazing, too. From the farmers to the businesspeople in town, he felt like he'd run into old friends whose sole purpose in life was to welcome weary people who didn't know what they were looking for. To top it all off, Noah now knew exactly what he wanted, and this was it.

Every day something new awaited him. One day he might get an emergency call that Mrs. Crowley's pampered poodle, Precious, had something in her paw. The next day he could find himself in Junior Whitmore's barn delivering a brand-new foal.

And on another day he could be up to his elbows in chickens, only to look up and see the most beautiful woman he'd ever laid eyes on. Emily was even more gorgeous than the picture on the Kimballs' mantel. To top it off, she was a Christian—couldn't ask for better than that.

꙳

"Need me for anything else?" Emily said.

"Noah went to get the rest of the chickens. But you can go on inside if you're tired."

"He's bringing more?"

Uncle Mel nodded. "Yup. Two more loads, in fact."

"Then I'm staying out here and helping until the last chicken is taken care of."

Aunt Sherry grinned, and she joined Uncle Mel as he closed the gap between himself and Emily. "You're a good girl, Emily. I don't know how it happened with all you went through, but we're mighty blessed to have you in our family."

"Daddy raised me right." Emily's eyes stung as she thought about how shocked her father had been when her mother—his wife—had chosen to take off when Emily needed her the most.

"You miss him, don't you?" Aunt Sherry asked.

Emily nodded. "More than you can ever imagine."

Her aunt tilted her head forward and raised her eyebrows. "So does Mel. Those two were closer than any brothers I've ever known."

"Daddy always talked about how much he appreciated both you and Uncle Mel."

"Don't go gettin' all sappy on me," Uncle Mel said. "We got work to do. No point in cryin' over something we can't do a thing about."

Before Emily had a chance to say another word, they heard the rumbling of Noah's truck on the bumpy road. "Let's go get those chickens so we can eat at a decent time."

They worked hard until the last chicken was securely in the barn. Aunt Sherry placed her hand in the middle of Emily's back. "Why don't you get cleaned up and rest for a few minutes before supper?"

"I can help," Emily argued.

"No, do what I said. Tomorrow you can help with meals. You've already done more than enough for today."

An hour later, the four of them—Aunt Sherry, Uncle Mel, Noah, and Emily—bowed their heads to thank the Lord for the meal in front of them. When Emily opened her eyes and saw Noah staring at her, she felt the blood rush to her cheeks. She offered a nervous smile, and he grinned right back at her.

She'd been through a long day, so after supper Noah left, and Emily excused herself to unpack. Her muscles ached from all the lifting, but she didn't mind. It sure beat being alone and in a dead-end job.

The next morning, Emily awoke to the sound of a rooster crowing. She blinked a couple of times before she remembered where she was. Then she smiled. As long as she was here with Aunt Sherry and Uncle Mel, all was good in her world. She slowly got out of bed and slipped on a fresh pair of jeans and a button-down shirt.

As she headed toward the kitchen, she took a deep breath and inhaled the aroma of fresh coffee brewing. Aunt Sherry turned around and held out a cup. "I hope you slept well."

"Like a baby," Emily replied. "How are the chickens?"

Aunt Sherry chuckled. "I trust you heard the crowing?"

"Yes."

"It's been awhile since we had roosters. I'd almost forgotten how much I enjoyed that sound."

Emily nodded. There was something comforting about a rooster crowing, and it sure beat the jolting ring of an alarm clock. She sat down at the table and stirred some sugar into her coffee.

"I told Noah we'd stop by his office on the way into town."

"How long has he been practicing here?"

"A little over a year." Aunt Sherry joined her. "That's long enough for all of us to appreciate what a hardworking young man he is." She smiled. "He goes to our church, too."

"That's nice." Emily squirmed and tried to think of a different subject. "I need to do a little shopping while I'm here."

After a quick bowl of cereal, the two of them took off in Aunt Sherry's station wagon. Emily appreciated how Aunt Sherry chattered nonstop. It kept her from having to make conversation. When they pulled into the parking lot of a strip mall with mostly vacant space, Emily turned to her aunt.

"What's this?"

Aunt Sherry pointed to the end of the shopping center. "That's Noah's clinic at the end. I like to park here, in case one of his elderly clients needs a closer spot."

Emily was surprised as she glanced around. She wasn't sure what she expected, but this wasn't it.

"He has some chicken feed that should tide us over until we can have some delivered," Aunt Sherry explained.

As soon as Emily opened the front door, she was accosted by a menagerie of farm animals—a goat, a couple of chickens, and the squealiest pig she'd ever heard.

two

Noah came around from behind the wall and tugged on the pig. "Sorry about that. Peewee likes visitors."

"Peewee?" Emily couldn't help but laugh.

"That's his name. Excuse me a minute while I tie him and Billy up in the back." He snapped his fingers. "C'mon, guys, you can't attack our friends." As Noah led the pig and goat to the back, his fingers tucked beneath both of their collars, the chickens scurried along right behind him.

Aunt Sherry winked at Emily. "Looks like Noah could use some help."

"Doesn't he have a receptionist?"

"Yes, Jillian comes in the afternoons, but she only works part-time."

Noah came back out, brushing his hands together. "Some of my patients are too nosy for their own good."

A clucking sound drew closer, capturing Emily's attention. "Looks like they can't stay away."

He snorted. "That's Helen. She hid when I put the other chickens in the cages. I know y'all are busy, so let's go get the feed, and you can be on your way."

The three of them loaded up some sacks of chicken feed by the back door. Aunt Sherry held up a finger. "Let me drive around so we don't have to carry them so far. Why don't you stay here, Emily?"

Emily nodded. After Aunt Sherry left, Noah bent over, picked up Helen, walked across the room, and unlocked the back door.

"They have interesting names," Emily said. "Any of them belong to you?"

17

Noah shook his head. "No, they're all flood rescues, and I'm waiting for some folks to come pick them up. These aren't from the same farm as the ones I brought over to your aunt and uncle's yesterday."

"I wondered about that." She looked down at the chicken, who'd made herself comfortable in Noah's arms. "Helen obviously likes you."

"Of course she does. Animals have a sense of who they can trust."

As if on cue, Helen belted out a loud squawk and flapped her wings. Noah laughed as he gently put her on the floor.

Emily squatted to get a better look at Helen. "Uncle Mel let me adopt a baby chick one summer when I stayed on their farm."

"That's what happened with Helen. After she fell out of the nest, the farmer's little girl found her and brought her inside, thinking the chicken might be hurt. At first she managed to hide her under the bed, but then she started making all kinds of noise. According to the child's mother, they tried putting her back with the other chickens, but she couldn't make it socially."

"I guess she must not have fit into their pecking order," Emily quipped.

Noah rolled his eyes. "That's pretty lame, but I like it."

"Oh, it gets better."

The back door slowly opened, and Aunt Sherry stepped gingerly inside. "Let's get the feed and head on home." She looked down at the chicken. "Is that Helen?"

"Yes. The Stantons had to be evacuated, and Chip Morris can't come until tomorrow, so I offered to take her until then."

Aunt Sherry leaned over and made some clucking noises before standing back up. "I bet she misses her family."

"I'm trying to keep her mind off them so she won't get homesick."

After they loaded the feed into the back of the station wagon, Emily and Aunt Sherry said good-bye to Noah and headed back to the farm. Emily suddenly found the whole situation hilarious, and she started laughing—softly at first, then in an uncontrollable fit.

"What's that all about?"

"A homesick chicken." She snorted through her giggles. "I've never heard of such a thing."

With that, Aunt Sherry started laughing so hard tears started falling, and she had to pull over to wipe her eyes. "It is funny."

"I wonder where she got the name Helen," Emily said between guffaws.

"That's a question for Noah." Aunt Sherry maneuvered the car back onto the highway leading to the farm. "But I'm not sure he knows."

"He fits in here pretty well, doesn't he?"

Aunt Sherry nodded. "We went through three different vets, all right out of college, and none of them could handle all the livestock. We're fortunate to have Noah. He spent some time working on farms around Georgia, and he discovered how much he enjoyed it."

"How did you find him?" Emily thought for a moment then amended her question. "Or should I say, how did he find you?"

"His family goes to church in Atlanta with one of Pastor Chuck's former classmates."

"I wonder why he wanted to get away from Atlanta."

Aunt Sherry shrugged but kept her focus on her driving. "Sometimes kids just need to find their own way out from under the shadow of their parents—especially after they've been adults for a while."

That made sense to Emily.

As soon as they got to the house, they fed the chickens. Emily offered to help with the other animals, but Aunt

Sherry said she preferred to do it alone. "Why don't you go through that box of pictures I have on the coffee table and see if there's anything you want copies of?"

Emily spent a few minutes looking through the pictures, but the memories were too painful. All the snapshots of her before she hit her teens included her mother—the woman she hadn't seen for years until her father died. By then they'd become strangers who could barely look at each other.

When Aunt Sherry came inside to start dinner, Emily stepped in with an offer of help and wouldn't take no for an answer. "Why don't you drive into town tomorrow?" Aunt Sherry said. "There's no point in hanging around here all day."

"I might do that."

"On your way back, you can stop by and pick up some medicine for Francine. She's gotten into something that's making her sick."

Emily grinned as she remembered how Francine the goat always had something wrong with her because she couldn't stay out of trouble. Last time Emily saw the goat—a couple of years earlier—she'd gotten tangled in some barbed wire. "What did she get into this time?"

"She's been getting into everything lately. Mel's been trying to figure out how to keep her contained, but Francine's an escape artist." She snickered. "We even tried tying her up, but she always manages to get loose."

Francine was one of Emily's favorite animals, mostly because she was such a rebel. While the other goats seemed satisfied hanging out inside the barn and playing in the small fenced yard beside it, Francine was a wanderer. Last time Emily visited, Francine actually made her way into the house—and no one had any idea how she'd gotten in.

The next morning, Emily got up and had breakfast before heading off toward town. She slowed down as she passed Pullman Square. Then she meandered through town until she found Ritter Park, wishing she'd brought her sketch pad.

Her stomach started growling around noon, so she stopped for fast food. She'd have to investigate the little town's art galleries on her next trip.

Aunt Sherry had said she'd call the clinic for the medicine, so all Emily would need to do was pick it up. When she opened the door, a young woman with curly blond hair who sat behind the reception desk greeted her.

"I'm here to pick up some medicine for my aunt's goat," Emily said.

The girl frowned. "Goat medicine?"

Emily nodded. "My aunt, Sherry Kimball, was supposed to call this morning."

"Oh, I just got here." She jumped up and came around from behind the counter. "Let me see if Dr. Blake knows anything about it. What's the name again?"

"Sherry Kimball."

Emily shifted her weight from one foot to the other and looked at the pictures on the wall, until she spotted movement in the doorway from the corner of her eye. When she looked up, Noah smiled at her.

"Hi, Emily. Did you need something?"

"Did Aunt Sherry get in touch with you about medicine for the goat?"

Noah frowned for a second then slowly shook his head. "I've been in surgery all morning, so if she called then, I wasn't available. Jillian has morning classes, so she doesn't get here until the afternoon. I assume you need something for Francine. Did Sherry tell you what kind of medicine she needed?"

"Something for her stomach. Aunt Sherry said she'd call," Emily replied.

Noah groaned. "Oh no, not again. I don't know why she likes to escape. She has it made there."

"I think she likes to do anything she's not supposed to."

Noah smiled and motioned for her to follow. "I'll fix you right up. Maybe I can come out there next weekend and help

Mel build a special pen that'll hold her."

Suddenly, a squealing grunt sounded from one of the examining rooms. Emily cast a questioning glance toward Noah.

He smiled. "That's Peewee. He hasn't gotten much attention lately."

"What's the deal with that pig? Why is he still here? I thought—"

Noah looked like he was ready to burst into laughter, but he managed to control himself with a half smile. "He wasn't one of the flood victims. They left yesterday afternoon. I'm waiting for the new owners to come pick Peewee up. He's part of the Vietnamese potbellied pig revolution."

Emily tilted her head. "The what?"

"Potbellied pigs. Their popularity surged, until people realized there was no guarantee they'd stay small."

Small was the last word she would use to describe Peewee. "Do you ever rest?" she asked.

The squeals grew more frantic, so Noah crossed the room and opened the door. Peewee came trotting in, his belly swaying with each step. Emily bent over and scratched behind Peewee's ears, eliciting delightful pig sounds.

Noah glanced down at her and laughed. "What do you mean by that? I rest."

"You're always working."

"I like what I do, so it doesn't seem like work." He pulled a bottle off the shelf and pointed to the directions taped on the side of it. "Give this to her as directed. It might take two of you—one to hold Francine still and the other to get her to swallow it."

"Thanks." Emily took the bottle without moving her gaze from Noah. "I'm really sorry about what I said. It was out of line."

"No offense taken. In fact, I think it's sweet that you noticed. I love animals, and I feel blessed that the Lord has allowed me to follow my dream of becoming a vet."

Emily offered a slight grin. "That must be nice—to know what you want and then be able to do it."

Noah tilted his head and studied her. "What do you want to do with your life, Emily Kimball?"

She glanced down then slowly lifted her gaze back to his. "I sure wish I knew. It seems there's not much of a demand for an art history major."

"You can teach."

"I'm not really qualified to teach." She shifted her focus away from him. "Besides, I'm not sure if that's what I really want."

"Why don't you try different things?" he asked.

"Like what?"

He glanced around the room. "Like maybe work with animals?"

"Work with animals?" she repeated.

He nodded. "Why not?"

"But where?"

Something electric sizzled between them. Noah looked up at the ceiling as he folded his arms and widened his stance. "How about right here? I could use some help in the mornings."

"Doing what?"

Noah gestured toward the reception area. "Answer phones, let me know when clients arrive, escort patients to the examining rooms, soothe upset pet owners, help bathe animals, take payments—"

"Are you serious?"

"Yep."

She squinted to get a different perspective. When he didn't budge, she finally nodded. "I think I just might consider it."

His eyebrows shot up in a look of pleasant surprise. He opened his mouth then shut it.

Maybe he didn't mean what he said. Sometimes people said things or made offers just to be polite. She was about to let him off the hook when a broad grin took over his face, crinkling the area around his dark brown eyes, melting her from the inside out.

"That would be awesome," he said, now with conviction. "When can you start?"

Emily let out a nervous chuckle. "I think I need to talk to Aunt Sherry and Uncle Mel first. I'm only supposed to be here for a few weeks."

"Even a few weeks would help." He gestured toward the reception desk. "I'm sure Jillian would appreciate not having a huge to-do stack waiting for her when she comes in every day." His expression grew more serious. "She has a lot going on in her life, and I don't want to add to her stress."

❧

After Emily had paid for Francine's medicine and left, Jillian snapped her fingers in front of his face. "Earth to Dr. Blake."

He jumped. "Oh, sorry. Did you say something?"

She smiled as she shook her head and sat back down at her desk. "You've got it bad."

"Huh?"

"You really like that girl, don't you?"

Noah blinked and turned to face her. "Yes, she seems very nice. Why?"

"She's more than nice. I saw how the two of you looked at each other." Jillian held up a stack of paperwork she hadn't yet filed. "You were right about needing some help around here. I sure hope she decides to take you up on your job offer."

"Yeah, me, too."

As Noah headed back to tend to one of the animals, he heard her mumble. It sounded strangely like, "Yeah, I bet you do."

He had a simple neutering surgery to do before his next appointment, so he prepped the table. As he scrubbed it down, Noah thought about how he'd blurted his offer to Emily before thinking about it. Yes, he needed more help, but he hadn't planned to add another person to the office for at least another month or so. It wasn't that he couldn't afford the help. He just didn't have the time to train anyone.

But now that he'd made the offer, he knew it was the right move. Since meeting Emily, he'd thought about her more than he should, something that hadn't happened since he and Tiffany had broken their engagement shortly after she moved to West Virginia. She'd rented an apartment in Huntington, and they'd spent quite a bit of time together at first. Then his new practice had taken so much of his energy, and she whined about feeling neglected. Suddenly she stopped complaining, so he thought everything was fine. Then he was blindsided when she announced that she'd met someone new and they were moving to Charleston. What surprised him most was that he wasn't all that disappointed. After he thought about how different life was between the posh Atlanta suburb of Dunwoody and the rural area he served in West Virginia, he knew she'd be miserable. But he loved every minute of his new life.

At first, he felt free from worrying about how Tiffany would adapt to the new life. He saw the split up as a sign that he and Tiffany weren't meant to be together. However, there were times when he got lonely, and he wondered if he'd made a mistake.

Until now, he hadn't given much thought to a love life, but there was something about Emily that sent his senses reeling—something he couldn't quite put his finger on. Sure she was pretty, but there were plenty of attractive women in town. She was smart and funny, too. But that wasn't all.

Noah had felt an unexpected zing in his heart when she didn't hesitate to pitch in with the chickens. Her genuine ease with the animals reminded him of how he'd always been. And it made her beyond attractive. Sometimes when their gazes met, he felt as though she was looking into the windows of his own soul. They had some kind of unspoken connection he'd never experienced with anyone.

The bell on the front door jolted him from his thoughts, so he turned around and glanced at the clock. *Whew.* It wasn't too late to start on the neutering before his appointment. He wanted to leave at a decent time so he could check on some of the animals he'd placed in the care of nearby farmers. His schedule had been turned upside down since the flood.

He was about to pull Festus, the Yorkie who'd been patiently waiting for his surgery, from the cage, when he heard a woman's voice and a little girl's wail. Noah patted Festus on the head, said, "Be a good boy. I'll be right back," and placed him back in the cage.

Jillian had her arms around the little girl, who held tight to a half-grown chicken. "I promise we'll take good care of her," the receptionist told her.

"No!" The little girl yanked the chicken away and started sobbing. "You can't have Pinky."

three

Noah assumed the woman next to the child was her mother, so he gestured for her to follow him. Once they were out of hearing distance, he stopped. "Why is Pinky here?"

The woman looked distraught. "We had no idea the baby chick would get so big. Gina wanted a pink Easter chicken, so we got her one." She swiped at the tear on her cheek. "The chicken isn't pink anymore, and she's obviously not a baby, and—I don't know what to do. We live in town, and we're not allowed to have farm animals in our apartment. The manager told us to get rid of the chicken, or else."

Noah groaned. The very thought of animals being sold as Easter presents had always been a sore spot with him.

"So you brought the chicken here for me to find it a home?"

She nodded. "If you can." After a sniffle, she added, "I heard you like chickens."

His jaw tightened, so he took a deep breath and slowly let it out. "I think I can find someone who'll take the chicken, but you need to understand that it's not okay to buy dyed baby chickens—no matter how much your child wants one."

"Yes, I know." She offered a slight smile of apology. "Gina was a very sick little girl, so we're guilty of spoiling her."

Although Noah didn't have children, he had been guilty of spoiling a few of his animals, so he nodded. "I know how that can happen. Let's go see if we can convince Gina to let go of her little friend."

When they got back to the reception area, Noah was pleasantly surprised to see that Emily had returned. She sat on one side of Gina, while Jillian sat on the other. They all had their hands on Pinky, who had started clucking in annoyance. Emily looked up at him as she stifled a smile.

"I think she's lonely," Emily offered as she turned back to the little girl.

Gina shrugged. "She's not lonely, 'cuz she has me."

Emily glanced over Gina at Jillian, who smiled and nodded. "Do you have any friends besides Pinky?"

The little girl frowned for a moment then nodded. "Lacy is my friend, and sometimes I play with Brooke in the next building."

Emily stroked the chicken then placed her hand on Gina's shoulder. "I think Pinky would like other chickens to play with."

Gina didn't waste any time shaking her head. "She can't. The manager of our apartment won't let us have chickens."

"I have an idea," Emily said. "Why don't you bring Pinky to my aunt and uncle's farm, and she can play with the chickens there?" She glanced up for reassurance from Noah.

He nodded and took the cue to join them. "That's a great idea. They have a whole barn full of chickens. Pinky will have all kinds of playmates there."

Everyone in the room held their breath while Gina pondered this idea. Finally she said, "Okay, we can see if Pinky likes any of those chickens. But I don't want to give her away."

Noah wasn't sure exactly what to do next, so he turned to Emily, hopeful that she'd have a suggestion. Once again the room grew quiet.

Finally Emily's shoulders relaxed. "I understand. Let's just give Pinky a chance to play with the chickens and see how things go, okay?"

Gina's face lit up. "Can I watch?"

"Yes, of course you can watch." Emily turned to Gina's mother. "Would you like to follow me to the farm?"

"Sure. We'll be glad to." The woman extended her hand to her daughter. "Come on, Gina." She turned back to Emily.

"We'll wait in the car. Take your time."

After they left, Noah looked relieved. "You just saved me. I had no idea how to handle the little girl."

"The only reason I knew what to do was because I had to give up a chicken when I was younger." His heart melted at the look of sympathy on her face. "Oh, I almost forgot. I think I left my cell phone on the counter when I paid for Francine's medicine."

Jillian walked over to the reception counter, got the phone, and brought it back to Emily. "Here ya go. I was so busy I didn't even see it."

"Thanks," Emily said as she pocketed the phone. "I guess I better head on out so Pinky can meet her new friends in the barn."

"Want me to call your uncle and let him know you're bringing a guest?" Noah offered.

Emily grinned. "That would be nice. Thanks! I'll give you my cell number, just in case."

As soon as Emily left, Noah picked up the phone and punched in Mel's number. It rang five times before the voice mail came on. He left a message and hung up.

"I'll be in surgery for a little while," he said. "If Mel calls back, tell him about the chicken."

Jillian gave him the thumbs-up sign. "Sure thing."

Festus was so happy to see Noah when he returned to the holding area that he licked all over Noah's hand and looked up at him, his tongue still hanging out of his mouth. Noah chuckled. "Sorry, little buddy. The things we do for the ladies."

Festus pulled his tongue into his mouth and cocked his head to one side. After a couple of seconds, he resumed his licking, until the anesthesia kicked in.

After the surgery was over, Noah gently put Festus in the recovery room then went back out to the reception area. "Have you heard from Mel yet?"

Jillian shook her head. "Not yet."

Noah tried again but to no avail. "Mel needs to carry a cell phone."

"I'm sure it'll be fine. After all, it's only one chicken we're talking about."

"Yeah, what's one more when you have a barn full of them?" Noah picked up the phone again. "I need to let Emily know I couldn't get hold of Mel."

ঽ

The instant Emily made the last turn toward the farm, she saw all the commotion. Aunt Sherry was running around the area by the barn, a pot in one hand and a spoon in the other, banging them together. Uncle Mel stood off to the side, one hand on his hip, the other rubbing the back of his neck.

And chickens were everywhere! Something had obviously happened, and the chickens were loose. She slowed down to try to figure out what to do about the little girl and her mother who'd followed her home.

Suddenly her phone chirped, so she flipped it open and said, "Hello?"

"I couldn't get in touch with Mel," Noah said. "I'm sure he won't mind taking on another chicken."

"He might not mind, but I'm not so sure about little Gina." Then she told Noah what she saw.

"Is there any way you can hold them off? I don't want to scare the child."

Emily glanced in her rearview mirror and saw Gina's mother pointing toward the barn. "No, I don't think so."

She heard Noah exhale. "Call me back if you need me."

"I think I can handle this, Noah. I understand that you feel responsible for all the animals in the county, but you need to let go. There are some things out of your control." The instant those words left her mouth, Emily couldn't believe she'd said them.

"Um—okay," he said. "I'll check with Mel later."

Emily felt bad about the brashness of her words, but she knew what it was like to worry about something out of her control. "Let me give you a call in a little while—after I find out what's going on and everything is settled."

He hesitated for a couple of seconds before he finally said, "Okay."

She pulled into the driveway with the car behind her still in her line of vision. At least Gina's mother hadn't freaked out and given up.

Aunt Sherry ran right over to her the instant she opened her car door. "Francine let the chickens out."

Emily looked at the barn then back at Aunt Sherry. "How did she do that?"

Her aunt shook her head. "To make a long story short, back when we still had chickens Francine used to follow Mel when he went to the barn to check on them. Since she seemed harmless and she didn't bother them, we didn't think anything about it when she wandered into the barn this afternoon."

"But how did she let the chickens out?"

By this time, Gina and her mother had joined them. Pinky rested in Gina's arms like a fashion accessory. Emily's mind instantly went into artist mode and imagined what a great portrait that would make.

Aunt Sherry glanced over at Gina then her mother before settling her gaze on Emily. "Would you like to introduce me to your friends before I go back and help Mel get the chickens back in the barn?"

Emily briefly told her aunt about Pinky. Gina held her chicken out so Aunt Sherry could see her better.

"She looks like a very nice chicken, Gina," Aunt Sherry said. "If you'd like to go on into the house, there's some fresh cobbler on the kitchen counter. It should be cool by now." Aunt Sherry nodded toward Emily. "Why don't you get them settled at the kitchen table, and I'll be in there in a few minutes. This won't take long."

Emily gestured for Gina and her mother to follow her. They'd gone about twenty feet when Francine the goat joined them.

"Mommy!" Gina shrieked, still holding on to Pinky.

"Francine is a nice goat," Emily said as she reached for one of Gina's hands and managed to gently wrest it free from Pinky. She guided the little girl's fingertips to Francine's back and slowly stroked the goat. "See? She's just like any other animal."

"Will she hurt Pinky?" Gina asked.

Since Emily wasn't sure about anything anymore, she didn't want to take a chance. "I've never seen her hurt chickens before, but why don't you hold on to Pinky until my aunt gets all the other chickens rounded up and back in the barn?"

They went inside, where Emily scooped some cobbler for Gina and her mother. When she turned around, she saw Noah standing at the kitchen door. Her heart made a flip.

"I couldn't stay away after I spoke to you on the phone," he said. "Let me go help Mel and Sherry, and I'll be right back."

He disappeared without another comment. As Emily set the bowls of cobbler down in front of her guests, Gina's mother grinned at her. "He seems like such a nice man. How long have you two been together?"

"Huh?"

"You and the vet? You *are* dating aren't you?"

Emily shook her head. "No, I'm sorry if I gave you the wrong impression. He takes care of all the animals around here, and my aunt sent me to Noah's Ark to pick up some medication for Francine."

Pinky let out a loud squawk then flapped her wings, nearly toppling the bowl in front of Gina. The girl's mother reached out and grabbed it in the nick of time.

And Emily was relieved that she didn't have to answer the question, but it shouldn't have bothered her at all. Somehow it seemed intrusive on her innermost thoughts.

Emily hopped up and put everyone's bowls in the sink. By the time she finished rinsing and putting them in the dishwasher, Aunt Sherry had come inside.

"We got 'em all back into the barn, thanks to Noah," she said as she stuck her hands under the faucet and washed them. "He and Mel are out there working up a solution to keep Francine out of the barn. We can't have her deciding to set the chickens free just because she likes the attention."

Gina held up Pinky. "My chicken likes attention."

Aunt Sherry grinned down at the little girl. "I think most animals do."

Gina's mother stood up. "I'm afraid we're imposing. If we can come back at another—"

"Nonsense," Aunt Sherry said. "You're definitely not imposing. We welcome guests. I just hate that y'all had to see us in such a flap."

Emily had to stifle a giggle. Gina looked at her and blinked.

Aunt Sherry spoke up again. "I understand you're looking for accommodations for Pinky." She dried her hands and crossed the room to where Gina and her mother stood. "Forgive my manners. I'm Sherry Kimball. I know your daughter is Gina, but I didn't catch your name."

The woman smiled. "Maria. Nice to meet you, Sherry. And yes, we'd like to find a nice home for Pinky. Our apartment complex isn't set up for farm animals."

Emily held her breath as all of them looked down at the little girl whose grip on Pinky had only tightened since they'd been there. Aunt Sherry reached out and stroked the bird on the head. "Pinky seems like such a nice chicken. Would you like to take her out to the barn and let her meet some other chickens?"

Gina glanced up at her mother, who nodded, then turned to face Aunt Sherry. "Can I meet them, too?"

"Of course you can. We have some mighty friendly chickens."

"Do they play together?" Gina asked.

"Sometimes. But mostly they sit around and cackle while they lay eggs."

Gina's eyes widened. "They lay eggs? Real eggs?"

Aunt Sherry reached down, placed her arm around Gina, and gently guided her to the door. "Yes, real eggs. In fact, there might even be some now. Wanna go out there and see if they left us any?"

Gina grinned. "Can I get them?"

Emily stood watching in amazement as Aunt Sherry led the little girl, still holding Pinky—only not so close as before—outside to the barn. She turned to Maria. "My aunt is wonderful with children. I used to love coming here when I was Gina's age."

"I'm so happy there's a place for Pinky," Maria said. "The apartment manager threatened to send her to a chicken-packing plant. That scared Gina half to death."

Emily shuddered. She couldn't imagine what must have gone through Gina's mind when he said that. "He sounds like a cruel man."

"You don't know the half of it."

They got outside in time to see Aunt Sherry and Gina disappearing into the barn. "Would you like to see the chickens, too?"

Maria looked skeptically at the wooden structure. "Do they bite? I mean, I'm used to Pinky and all, but she's the only chicken I've ever been around."

"No. Some of them make a little noise, but I've never seen one bite anyone."

"I guess," Maria said softly. "It would be nice to see where Pinky will be living."

A single bulb hanging in the middle of the massive structure lit the center of the barn and cast a gentle glow around the walls, leaving darkened corners. Chicken crates and coops covered one wall of the barn, while the other side was lined with hay.

"What do you think?" Emily asked. "Is this what you expected?"

Maria's nose crinkled. "It smells weird. Kind of earthy."

"That's the hay." Emily took a deep breath. "I've always loved that smell." She laughed. "It would stink if Uncle Mel didn't keep it so clean."

"Mommy, look! Pinky has her own bed, and she likes it!"

Maria flashed a smile at Emily before scurrying over to her daughter, who stood beside a coop. Pinky had settled down and seemed perfectly content.

"That's so sweet!" Maria said.

Aunt Sherry reached for Gina's hand. "Now let's go gather some eggs. You want to take some home with you?"

"Can we, Mommy?"

"If Mrs. Kimball doesn't mind, it's fine with me."

Aunt Sherry found a basket and helped Gina check the coops for eggs, while Emily chatted with Maria.

"Your aunt is a very sweet woman," Maria whispered. "I'm glad Pinky has a nice place to stay."

Emily nodded. "She'll be just fine."

A few minutes later, Gina headed toward the door of the barn carrying a basket filled with eggs. She stopped off at Pinky's coop, leaned over, and whispered something then caught up with the adults. "I told her to behave and not run away, even if the goat tells her to."

After Gina and her mother left, Emily hugged Aunt Sherry. "Thanks so much. Oh, by the way, do you mind if I hang out here for a few extra weeks? Noah needs some help at the clinic, and I sort of—well. . ."

Sherry smiled and nodded. "He already told me he wants you to work mornings. And I'd love to have you here as long as you want to stay."

"Thank you so much!"

"We have everything under control." The booming voice made both women jump.

Emily turned around and saw the look of amusement in Noah's eyes and the slight grin on his lips, and she felt the heat rush to her face. Why did he have to be so attractive? "You startled me!"

He shoved his hands into his pockets but kept smiling. "At least you're still breathing."

The combination of his rugged good looks, the way he cared about his work, and the mischievous look on his face made her wonder if he could hear her raspy breath. She swallowed hard and forced herself to deeply inhale then slowly let it out.

"Yes, I'm still breathing." She mimicked his stance and put her hands in the pockets of her own jeans then stared directly into his eyes. "By the way, when did you want me to start working at the clinic?"

four

Noah stifled the temptation to tell her *now*. Immediately. He didn't want to spend another minute away from her.

"How about tomorrow?" he blurted.

Sherry didn't give Emily a chance to speak. "Isn't that a little soon?"

"Yeah, don't rush the girl," Mel piped up as he joined them in the kitchen. "She probably has a dozen things to do to get ready for this job."

"Like what?" Sherry asked.

Mel tilted his head back and belted out a hearty laugh. "Exactly. Why can't she start tomorrow?"

Noah couldn't hide his amusement. He rubbed his chin for a moment then looked at Emily. "When would you like to start?"

All eyes were on her as she stood there trying to figure out what to do. Finally she held out her hands and shrugged. "There's really no reason I can't start tomorrow, unless Aunt Sherry has something she wants me to do around here."

"We're good," Sherry said. "Do you need her, Mel?"

"Nah, not really." Mel turned and faced Noah. "If she wants to start tomorrow, I think it's a fine idea. It'll keep her from being bored."

"I'm not bored," she said. "There's always something to do around here."

Noah couldn't help comparing Emily to Tiffany. Emily was the type of woman who could find something to do no matter where she was, while Tiffany had to have her hair stylist, manicurist, and favorite designer shops to keep her entertained.

"Since you're starting right away," Sherry said, "why don't

the two of you go somewhere and discuss everything?"

Emily cast a questioning glance toward her aunt. Then she turned to Noah. "Do we need to discuss anything?"

Sherry jumped in again. "Sure you do. Things like hours, salary, and dress code."

Noah smiled. "This is strictly part-time—at least for now. Jillian comes in around one most afternoons, and she really needs the work, so any morning hours would be appreciated." He made an apologetic face. "I can't afford more hours than that."

"I understand. Is it okay if I wear jeans?" Emily asked. "I mean, since I'll be working around animals and all."

"Sure." Noah gestured toward his own clothes. "That's what I wear most of the time." He paused for a moment before adding, "I haven't thought about salary yet. Why don't we discuss that tomorrow when you come in?"

"Okay, that's fine," Emily said. "It's not like I expect to get rich or anything."

Quite unlike Tiffany, he thought. He extended his hand. "Shake on it?"

As she reached out and placed her hand in his, he felt the soft warmth in her slender fingers. She had quite a firm handshake, but there was no question about her femininity, which caused a stir in his heart.

Mel rubbed his hands together and turned to his wife. "Looks like this will work out for everyone. We get to have our niece here with us, Noah gets help at the clinic, and Emily will have something to do while she's here and some money in her pocket."

Noah took a step back. "Hey, folks, I need to get back to the clinic. Anything else I can do while I'm here?"

"Let me walk you to your truck," Mel said. "I have something I'd like to discuss before you leave."

❧

The instant the men left the house, Aunt Sherry turned to

Emily. "Are you sure you want to do this? We didn't expect you to work while you were here."

Emily nodded. "I really don't mind."

"I didn't think you did. I just wanted to make sure." The twinkle in her eye was a giveaway she was up to something.

"Is there something you're not telling me, Aunt Sherry?"

"Whatever do you mean?"

"Are you plotting something?"

Aunt Sherry flipped her hand at the wrist and clicked her tongue. "Must you always be so suspicious of me?"

Emily giggled. "You have a way of making things happen."

"Yes, I do, don't I?" Her smug expression left no doubt in Emily's mind something was going on, and she wouldn't find out until her aunt was good and ready to let her know.

"I guess you probably wouldn't tell me if you had something up your sleeve."

"That's right," Aunt Sherry replied, grinning. "But there is one thing I want you to think about, since you're planning to take a job. You love art so much that you might want to consider applying at one of the art galleries in Huntington."

"I'm just doing this to help Noah."

"Good girl."

"Besides," Emily added. "I really do love animals, and I think it'll be fun working with them."

"Let's start supper. We've had a big day, and I don't want you doing everything by yourself."

As they worked in the kitchen, they discussed how little their schedule would change. "With you working mornings, you can run errands on your way home—that is, if you don't mind."

"Of course I don't mind. And I can still help out with chores in the afternoon."

Aunt Sherry stopped chopping and looked up at Emily. "You've always enjoyed farm chores."

Emily nodded. "It doesn't seem like work to take care of

animals and tend to the garden. It's more fun than anything."

"That's the way your uncle and I feel. Unfortunately your father didn't like farming. He hated getting his hands dirty, and so did your mama."

The mention of her mother made Emily pause. "Mama didn't like much of anything."

"I'm sorry I brought her up, sweetie. If you'd rather not talk about her—"

"No, that's okay. It's been long enough—it doesn't hurt as much."

"Maybe one of these days she'll come around," Aunt Sherry said. "I hope you find it in your heart to forgive her when she does."

"I've already forgiven her." Emily cleared her throat and thought for a moment, trying to remember exactly when she'd taken that major step. Her daddy had told her that when he and her mama first got married, they'd dreamed of having a little girl just like her mama. When Emily came along, they were elated. Her mama dressed her up in the frilliest dresses and took her along on shopping trips. But Emily hadn't truly found joy until she was old enough to spend summers on the farm with Aunt Sherry and Uncle Mel. "It really hurt when she first left, but Daddy was always there for me, no matter what. I think Mama's the one who's suffering the most," she said softly. "At least that's what Daddy once said."

"He's right, you know. I just hope what your mother did won't keep you from falling in love one of these days."

Emily let out a nervous chuckle. "It's not like the men are lining up to be with me."

"All it takes is one," Aunt Sherry reminded her. "One good man who loves the Lord."

Emily's thoughts instantly went to Noah. She already knew he went to church, but based on experience, she also knew that going to church didn't make a man a Christian.

She opened her mouth to ask Aunt Sherry, but she quickly

clamped it shut. She didn't want to make her aunt think she had a desire for anything but employment from Noah.

"In spite of his privileged upbringing, Noah's one of the humblest Christian men I've ever met," Aunt Sherry said.

Now when she heard that, Emily's curiosity got the best of her. "What do you mean *privileged*?"

"He lived in one of the swankiest neighborhoods in a suburb of Atlanta. His father still has a veterinary practice there, and he treats cats and dogs worth more than some people's monthly salary around here."

Emily frowned. "How do you know all this?"

Aunt Sherry smiled and placed her hand on Emily's shoulder. "A group of us spent quite a bit of time getting to know Noah. We wanted the best vet to take care of our animals—from our livestock to our pets. We liked the fact that Noah not only helped his dad for a while but that he worked on different farms around Atlanta."

"How did y'all convince him to come?"

"We didn't. After the interview process, he brought his dad and showed him around to get a different perspective. His father said he wished it was him instead of Noah."

"But I thought—"

Aunt Sherry nodded. "Noah's father told Mel that all the money in the world can't make a man happy. His pampered patients are treated better than humans in some parts. The man has integrity, and he won't abandon his practice, but he encouraged his son to follow what he knew was right." She clicked her tongue. "He wanted Noah to work with him, but he also wanted his son to be happy."

Emily admired Noah even more. "I'm glad it all worked out so well."

"There's only one thing that saddened us at the time though," Aunt Sherry said, the corners of her mouth turning down. "He had a very pretty young woman with him, and we all thought they'd be getting married and settling here."

Emily's heart landed with a thud. "A pretty woman?"

"Yes, but she didn't like it here. Seems we don't have enough of the finer things in life that she's used to."

"So what happened to her?"

"She sort of faded away." Aunt Sherry resumed her task and continued talking. "If you ask me, it was all for the better. Noah didn't seem too fazed by her decision. Mel thinks he might have even been relieved. Some women require so much upkeep it's hard to do anything worthwhile."

Emily tried hard to imagine Noah with a high-maintenance woman, but she couldn't wrap her mind around it. That didn't seem like his type. He was handsome and obviously committed to what he did, but she pictured him as more of a rugged sort.

Aunt Sherry coughed and got her attention. "I think he's lonely."

"Why do you think that?"

"I don't know. Maybe because all he ever does is work and go to church. I don't think the man has gone out just for fun since he's lived here."

Emily knew what that was like. But Aunt Sherry didn't need to know that.

"What time is church on Sunday?"

Aunt Sherry grinned. "Changing the subject, huh? That's fine. I understand. Church is at ten."

Later that night, Emily got out her outfit for the next day. She decided on dark-washed jeans because they looked nicer than her everyday jeans. Then she hung her coral-colored, collared T-shirt on the closet door. A lightweight khaki jacket and her newer sneakers would complete the ensemble.

As she stepped back for a good look at her clothes, she couldn't help but wonder if Noah would even notice what she wore. And if he did, would he compare her to his former girlfriend? She shook herself and forced different thoughts. It didn't do a bit of good to harbor notions of her boss that were totally inappropriate.

The next morning she awoke to the sounds of her aunt and uncle milling around the house. They'd always been early risers—most of the time before dawn. She flung her legs over the side of the bed and got up, rubbing the sleep from her eyes.

She showered, got dressed, and applied a light touch of makeup before sauntering into the kitchen, where the aroma of fresh coffee welcomed her. Uncle Mel had just sat down at the table with his coffee mug and a newspaper in front of him.

"Good morning, sunshine," Aunt Sherry said. "Eggs and bacon or cereal and fruit?"

"I'll just pour myself a bowl of cereal, thanks."

Uncle Mel looked up from his paper. "Nervous?"

She wanted to say *no, not at all*, but that would be lying. Instead, she shrugged and scrunched her face. "Just a little."

"That's normal." He patted the table. "Grab some coffee and have a seat."

A half hour later Emily was on her way to town for her first day on the job at the vet clinic. Throughout school, she'd had no idea what she wanted to do with her life, but she never would have imagined being a receptionist for a veterinarian.

The light was on in the clinic when she arrived, but it was still half an hour before the posted opening time. Emily shoved on the door, but since it was locked, she cupped her hands and looked to see if anyone was there.

The moving shadows beyond the reception area let her know someone was there, so she knocked and waited. Noah appeared and let her in.

"I'll get you a key later." Noah gestured toward the reception desk. "After you put your things down, we can take a tour."

Emily was impressed with Noah's organization and his obvious compassion for animals. All the smaller animals had toys and blankets from home in their cages to comfort them with a sense of familiarity.

"I try not to keep them in cages any longer than necessary," he said.

Emily looked behind the door. "Where's the rest of the greeting committee?"

Noah tilted his head and frowned. "Greeting committee?"

"Peewee."

"Oh, him." He glanced at the clock behind her then laughed. "He's been picked up."

Noah continued with his tour, working his way from the back of the clinic to the front. "C'mon, let me show you what to do when someone comes in. We have all our files on the computer, and it's a simple program with easy-to-navigate screens."

It took all of ten minutes for her to understand how to pull up a patient's file and do what she needed. Noah explained how he had a tight schedule of caring for smaller animals in the clinic and visiting the nearby farms. No wonder he didn't have much of a social life. There wasn't a spare moment in his day.

"Jillian should be a few minutes early today. You can stick around until one, or you can leave."

"Why don't I run out and have a key made when she gets here?" Emily offered. "That way you won't have to take the time."

"That'll be great, if you don't mind."

As their gazes locked, Emily felt as though the bottom had fallen out of her stomach. The chemistry between them was so strong that she wondered if he felt it, too.

He backed up. "I have to prep one of the rooms for my first patient. If you need me, just let me know."

She went around behind the counter to put some distance between them and sat down in the chair. "I'm sure I'll be fine."

Over the next four hours that morning, Emily met a half

dozen dogs, a pair of vocal cats who obviously wanted to be anywhere but where they were, a ferret, a baby squirrel monkey named Punky, and a miniature pony named Razzle Dazzle. She didn't have a chance to look at the clock all morning.

Jillian walked in shortly after noon and dropped her handbag beside Emily's. "How was your first day on the job?"

"Busy." Emily stood up so Jillian could take over. "Where's the best place to have a key made? I told Noah I'd do that before I left for the day."

Jillian handed Emily her key to the clinic and told her where to go. Emily stepped outside and offered a quick prayer of thanks. The morning had gone by much too quickly, and she'd enjoyed every moment of it.

After she had a copy of the key, she returned Jillian's. Noah thanked her and asked if she planned to return the next day.

"Of course," she replied. "Why wouldn't I?"

Noah laughed. "This place can be a little crazy sometimes. I'm glad Punky didn't scare you away."

Jillian's eyes lit up. "Punky was here? He is so adorable!"

Emily agreed. "His expressions are priceless. You should have seen his face when he saw Noah."

"I can imagine," Jillian said. "Last time he was here, he didn't want to leave. He wrapped his arms around Noah, and we had to pry his little fingers loose."

"I heard he pitched a temper tantrum in the parking lot," Noah added, shaking his head. "Monkeys can be a handful."

Jillian turned to Emily. "In case you haven't already figured it out, Noah prefers farm animals."

As cute as Punky was, Emily agreed with Noah. She wasn't sure how to act with Punky.

The phone rang, and Jillian answered it. She listened, mumbled a few words, then hung up. Noah and Emily exchanged a glance, then Noah turned to Jillian.

"Who was that?"

Jillian shrugged. "Wrong number."

Emily thought that was odd because, although Jillian had only been on the phone a few moments, it was longer than she should have spent with a wrong number.

۞

The next couple of days at the clinic went by just as quickly as the first. Each night during dinner she entertained Aunt Sherry and Uncle Mel with tales of the animals' antics.

"You like working there, don't you?" Uncle Mel asked.

She nodded. "I love it, but I also know it's temporary."

Her aunt and uncle exchanged a quick glance before Aunt Sherry turned back to her. "You know everything in this life is temporary, but the Lord wants us to enjoy our work. We want you to know that you're welcome to stay with us as long as you feel comfortable here."

A lump formed in Emily's throat. "I appreciate that."

Noah had told her she didn't need to go in to work on Saturday, but she didn't want to miss anything; she went for a couple of hours, and he told her he was glad she had. When Sunday morning arrived, Emily slept an extra hour, until it was time to get up and get ready for church.

As they pulled into the parking lot, she spotted Noah standing on the church steps. Her heart skipped a beat.

"I told him to sit with us," Uncle Mel said. "I hope you don't mind."

Emily didn't have a chance to respond, since her aunt and uncle were out of the car and halfway across the parking lot by the time she got out of the car. Noah shook Uncle Mel's hand and hugged Aunt Sherry before meeting Emily's gaze with a wide grin.

Throughout the service, Emily couldn't forget Noah's presence beside her. He held the hymnal so she could see the words, which gave them a physical closeness that made her tingle. During the sermon, Noah casually draped an arm over the back of the pew, making her feel protected and warm.

Once church ended, Noah walked them to their car. "You've been a huge help at the clinic. I'm glad you agreed to work with me."

"I don't mind."

Uncle Mel laughed out loud. "That's an understatement. I've never seen my niece this happy since she was a little girl."

Emily felt the heat rise to her cheeks. She glanced over at Noah, and he winked.

"Why don't you come on over to the house in an hour or so?" Aunt Sherry asked. "I have a big dinner planned."

Noah appeared conflicted as he glanced around at the three of them. Emily wasn't sure what was going on in his mind as his chest rose and fell with each breath.

The sound of a car approaching captured their attention. A sheriff's department cruiser came to a stop not far from where they stood.

When the officer got out and headed straight toward them, Emily saw Noah's forehead scrunch. "Who's that?" Emily asked.

"My buddy Dwayne, but I don't think this is a personal visit." Noah turned toward the police officer. "Everything okay, Dwayne?"

"Nah, not really. Your alarm triggered a call that someone was breaking into your clinic. By the time I got there, they were gone, but the door was wide open. Alarm from the controlled substance cabinet must've scared 'em off."

five

"I better get on over there, then." Noah turned to Emily. "Looks like I have an emergency to attend to."

Emily's heart raced as she glanced back and forth between Noah and Dwayne, the police officer. Noah's clinic had been broken into, yet both men moved at their standard pace.

"Want me to go with you?" she asked.

When Noah shook his head, she saw the lines that had instantly formed on his face. She felt a combination of relief that he was worried and concerned about the break-in.

Uncle Mel grabbed her hand and tugged her back. "We better let them handle it. Let's get on home." He turned to Noah. "Stop by the house after you finish dealing with this."

On the way to the farm, Uncle Mel and Aunt Sherry discussed all the possibilities of why someone would want to break into Noah's Ark. "Could be all the fancy equipment he has," Aunt Sherry speculated.

Uncle Mel snorted. "I suspect it's worse than that. I bet it's the drugs."

"But those are for the animals," Emily said. "Why would someone steal animal drugs?"

Her uncle glanced at her in the rearview mirror. "Animal narcotics are powerful. Put those in the hands of a serious drug user or dealer, and you've got a dangerous situation."

The thought of a person breaking into a vet's office for drugs had never crossed Emily's mind before. "I sure hope they catch whoever did it."

Aunt Sherry turned and faced Emily. "This isn't the first time we've seen this."

Emily didn't miss Uncle Mel's eye signal. "What happened before?"

"We might as well tell her, Mel. It's not like it affects her or anything."

Her uncle thought it over for a couple of seconds before he finally bobbed his head. "Okay, Sherry, go ahead."

Aunt Sherry took a deep breath before she began. "The last vet we had was excellent—but not quite as good as Noah, of course. He was wonderful with the animals, and he worked tirelessly. Then something snapped, and he started showing up late. Once when he came out here to help deliver one of the goats, I thought he was drunk."

"That's terrible."

Her aunt nodded. "Yes, it was rather frightening because Daisy needed help that we couldn't give her. The only reason we called him was because the kid was breech."

"Daisy seems okay now."

"She's fine, and the kid is fine. But that's only because Pastor Chuck just happened to stop by for a visit. He helped Mel deliver it, while Marvin—that's the vet—slept in the corner of the barn."

"So what happened then?"

Uncle Mel and Aunt Sherry exchanged a glance. "We found out later he wasn't drunk. Mel called the police and told them Marvin had driven drunk to our house, so they sent someone out to pick him up. When they did the blood test, they found a high level of narcotics in his blood."

Emily's face tightened as her eyebrows shot up. "He was taking the animals' drugs? That's insane."

"That's one of the reasons the community got involved in the search for a new vet. We all agreed that we needed to do a background check on the prospects."

Uncle Mel snorted. "That didn't sit too well with some of them. We lost a couple who said they didn't appreciate their privacy being invaded. In fact, one of them threatened to sue.

But we stuck to our guns and didn't let them bully us."

Aunt Sherry touched Uncle Mel's arm before she took over. "When we heard about Noah through the pastor, we actually went to visit him. I guess I told you most of this already. Thankfully everyone agreed that this was a good fit for Noah."

"Everyone," her uncle added, "but that prissy girlfriend of his." He made a face. "After she left, Noah seemed miserable, but I think he sees that he's better off without her. All she cared about was the money he could make so she could gallivant around town in her fancy clothes and uppity ways."

"Now, Mel, you know it's not right to judge people."

In spite of the seriousness of the conversation, Emily couldn't help but smile. Aunt Sherry was the quintessential Christian woman. She stood behind her faith in actions and thoughts.

Uncle Mel cringed and ducked. "I'm just sayin'. . ."

They rode most of the rest of the way home in silence, until they reached the road right before the last turn. Aunt Sherry looked at Uncle Mel. "I hope Noah plans to stop by later for dinner."

"Oh, I'm sure he will. When was the last time that boy turned us down for Sunday dinner?"

Aunt Sherry turned around and winked at Emily. "He has good taste in food."

Ten minutes later, the three of them had changed out of their church clothes and headed outside to tend to the animals. After all the chickens, goats, and cows were fed, Aunt Sherry swiped her sleeve across her forehead. "I need to go in and take a shower before I start cooking."

"Need any help?" Emily asked.

Aunt Sherry glanced at Uncle Mel then shook her head. "Why don't you help Mel finish up out here? I'll put you to work after you're done and cleaned up."

As soon as she went inside, Uncle Mel stopped working

and got her attention. "Any chance you'll stick around here?"

"You mean permanently?"

Uncle Mel paused, narrowed his eyes, then shook his head. "Well, nothing's permanent, but for a while."

"I might," Emily replied without hesitation. "But I don't want to impose on you and Aunt Sherry."

"Don't go gettin' the notion you're imposing. We already told you to stay with us as long as you want. This house is plenty big."

"You miss having the family all here, don't you?"

He gave her a sad look that melted her heart. "Yeah, that's the thing about kids growing up. They start new lives, and it's not always close to home. We never expected Saul to move halfway across the country. Meredith and Jennifer, yes, but not the baby."

"At least they're happy, and you know they love you."

Uncle Mel pondered that for a moment. "I think your mama loved you. She just didn't know how to cope with the stress of having a teenager."

"I might have been a little trouble, but I really wasn't all that bad."

"I know you weren't, Emily. In fact, you were the best-behaved kid we knew—including your three cousins." He grinned. "Sherry and I always suspected you went overboard in trying to please all the adults in your life because you were afraid of running them off."

He was so right! Emily had always blamed herself for her mama leaving, and sometimes she had lay awake at night, watching the door, praying that her daddy wouldn't take off in the dark.

"Here, take this rake and finish strewing the straw, then go on in and help Sherry. She's goin' all out on today's dinner, and I'm sure she could use an extra pair of hands to finish up."

Emily did as she was told. As soon as she stepped out of the shower adjoining her bedroom, she heard voices from down the hall—Aunt Sherry's, Uncle Mel's, and. . .she was pretty sure that was Noah talking, but the tone was so soft she wasn't positive.

Fortunately her aunt and uncle had always been casual, including during special meals. She pulled on a pair of her newest jeans and a knit baby-doll shirt. For an extrafeminine touch, she added a necklace with a butterfly pendant.

By the time she got to the kitchen, Uncle Mel had gone to clean up. Aunt Sherry stood at the counter rolling out dough for biscuits, and Noah was stirring the gravy. They both glanced up when she entered the room.

"Was it bad?" Emily asked. "Did they take anything?"

Noah shook his head. "No, but not for lack of trying. It's illegal to leave certain medications out. I have them under lock and key—and behind that, another security lock with an extra alarm."

"Good thinking," she replied. "How did they get in?"

"That's a good question. Either someone is very good at picking locks, or they had access to a key."

"Who else has a key?"

"That's where I'm puzzled. Right now, there are only four of us who have a key—you, Jillian, Jeffrey the maintenance man, and me. You and I were in church when this happened, and Jeffrey is out of the country."

Emily felt the blood drain from her face. "You don't think Jillian—"

"No," he said, interrupting her. "At least I hope Jillian wouldn't do something like that, but I do need to find out if she gave the key to someone else."

"Why would she do that?"

"Maybe she was busy and asked a friend to feed the kittens."

"Kittens?"

Noah pursed his lips as he laid the spoon on the plate. Then he turned around, folded his arms, and leaned against the counter. "I guess she must not have told you about the stray cat and kittens we feed. The mother cat started coming around a couple of months ago, and we felt sorry for her because she was obviously homeless and hungry. I've tried to catch her to spay her, but she runs off when I get near her. Next thing we knew, she had a litter in one of the bushes behind the clinic. We've been waiting for their mother to wean them so we can find homes for them."

"Why don't you bring them all over here?" Aunt Sherry asked.

Noah chuckled. "That might have been an option before the flood, but I don't think it's a good idea with all those chickens you're taking care of. Besides, this cat's very skittish, and although she'll come close, she keeps a distance of about ten feet."

Aunt Sherry put the last biscuit on the pan and brushed her hands together. "If you have trouble placing any of those kittens, we'll take them."

"Oh, we will, will we?"

The sound of Uncle Mel's voice made Aunt Sherry turn. "I miss having a house pet."

Uncle Mel laughed. "I know you do. That's fine. We can have one kitten."

"Two?" Aunt Sherry made a puppy dog face.

"Okay, two." He rolled his eyes then turned to Noah. "I'm too easy."

After the biscuits were done, they sat down and said a blessing before filling their plates. Emily expected talk to be all about the break-in at the animal clinic, but the subject never even came up again.

Emily looked around the table after they finished eating. She couldn't believe how much they had left.

"I like having leftovers," Aunt Sherry explained.

"Sherry, there's enough food for a family of five to have leftovers for a week." Uncle Mel looked at Noah. "She likes to keep us well fed."

Aunt Sherry grinned at Noah. "I'll just send some home with you. I'm sure you'll be hungry later."

He pushed back from the table and carried his plate to the sink. "I'd love to take you up on that, but I'm afraid I can't. I have to go back to the police station and talk to Dwayne before he goes off duty."

"Want Emily to come along?" Uncle Mel asked.

Noah glanced at Emily, making her heart skip a beat. "Would you like to join me?"

She thought for a few seconds and realized he'd have to drive her all the way back to the farm, so she slowly shook her head. "I better not. I have to do some laundry and get ready for the week."

Aunt Sherry cast a stern glance her way, but Emily turned her head. She didn't need matchmaking at the moment, and Noah had more important things on his mind.

The next morning, Emily went off to work with no idea what she'd find. Hopefully the perpetrator had been caught, but she was fairly certain if that were the case, she would have heard something by now.

Emily turned into the parking lot and drove past the spaces near the front door, leaving them for patients. As she got out of her car, she inhaled deeply, closed her eyes, and said a silent prayer as she slowly released her breath.

Every light in the clinic was on as she pushed the door open. About a second and a half later, Noah popped around from behind the wall. When he saw that it was her, he grinned.

"I'd like you to meet Kingston," he said as he led a black, full-grown, floppy-eared, flap-jawed, Great Dane on a short red leash. "He's going to hang out with us until we find out who tried to get in."

Emily knelt beside the dog, making him taller than her. She scratched behind his ear as she glanced up at Noah. "Who does Kingston belong to?"

"Joel Zimmerman. He's been trying to find someone to take care of him while he travels to Europe. When he first asked me if I knew of anyone, I couldn't think of a soul, but I said I'd take Kingston if nobody else would." He grinned. "After what happened. . ." His voice trailed off.

"I thought you had the drugs under lock and key." Emily stood, folded her arms, and waited for an answer.

"That's right, but since I don't know who came in here, I don't know what they'd be willing to do to get the drugs. What if they come back?" He snapped his fingers to beckon Kingston, and the dog eagerly obeyed.

"Good point," Emily agreed as she smiled at the dog. "Kingston seems like a sweet dog, but I don't think anyone will mess with us as long as he's here."

Noah glanced at his watch. "I have two annual checkups first thing this morning, then I have to go out for some farm visits. Kingston can stay here with you."

"Will you be back before I leave?" she asked.

He nodded. "I should be. If not, I'll call you." After a short pause, he added, "I'll call you anyway. I'm concerned about leaving you here alone."

Emily pointed to Kingston. "I won't be alone."

As if on cue, the dog left Noah's side and plopped his rear beside Emily's feet. She placed her hand on his shoulder, and he leaned against her hip, looking up at her with the most soulful, adoring eyes, his jaw flapping open. He let out a long sigh that sounded like that of an old man. Both Emily and Noah laughed.

"I don't think he'll let anything happen to you," Noah said. "He's already enamored."

"Yes, I do have a way with animals." She leaned over and cupped Kingston's face in her hands. "You'll protect me, won't you, boy? You'll chase anyone who comes after me, and you'll lick 'em to death."

The door opened, signaling the beginning of Noah's busy

day. After Noah left for his farm visits, Emily worked steadily, filing, answering the phone, scheduling appointments, and processing client bills that were long overdue. She could see that Noah made a good living, but he could do much better if people would pay on time. He didn't seem to worry about it, so she didn't need to concern herself with it either.

Noah called her midmorning and shortly before lunch. The second time, he said he wouldn't be back until midafternoon, but she could go ahead and tell Jillian what had happened. Disappointment flooded her as she hung up. It wasn't likely she'd see him again until the next morning, and that wouldn't be for long since he was booked with farm visits most of the week.

A few minutes before one o'clock, she started clearing away the desk, getting it ready for Jillian. But one o'clock came and went, and Emily's replacement still hadn't arrived. That was strange. Jillian was early most days, and the one time she ran late, she'd called. She tried Jillian's cell phone, but it went directly to voice mail without ringing. Emily didn't want to call and alert Noah because he was so busy.

At two thirty Noah walked in and did a double take then smiled. "Can't stay away, huh? Where's Jillian?"

Emily shrugged. "She didn't come in."

"Did you call her?" He frowned.

"I tried her cell phone, but it didn't even ring. Want me to try again?"

"No, let me see if I can find her mother's number. I'll see if she knows where Jillian is." Noah pointed to the computer. "Can you pull up my address book in Outlook?"

Emily got the information Noah needed, and he called Jillian's mother. As he chatted with the woman, Emily saw his look of concern deepen. Then he hung up and ran his fingers through his hair.

"That's odd. She said her daughter hasn't been home in several days, but she doesn't seem worried at all. In fact, she hasn't seen Jillian since Thursday night."

"She was here Friday."

"Yeah, I know," he said. "So she left here and didn't go home. Something's not right."

six

Emily studied Noah and wondered if he'd made any connection between Jillian being missing and the break-in. After all, there were only a few keys to the front door, and it had been established that entry wasn't forced.

Noah frowned as he pondered what to do. Emily had to come up with something—a way to help.

"Tell you what," she said. "Why don't I call around and see if anyone has seen her?"

He slowly nodded. "I'll call her mother back and get the numbers of some of her friends."

"Do you have any idea where she likes to go when she's not here or in class?"

He shook his head. "No idea whatsoever. I hired her because she was in college and needed some money. The pastor brought her to me." The worry etched on his face tugged at her heart.

Emily smiled to try to soothe him. "I'm sure everything will be okay. If something bad happened, we would have heard by now."

"I hope you're right."

They devoted the next hour to getting contact information. After Emily assured him she'd be fine at the clinic with Kingston by her side, Noah took off looking for Jillian in all the places her mother said she might be. What puzzled Emily was why the woman wasn't more worried about her own daughter.

As soon as Noah left, Emily called her aunt to let her know she'd be late. "Jillian didn't come in, so I'm filling in for her."

"Oh dear," Aunt Sherry said. "I hope she's not sick.

Something awful's going around. I bet she caught it at school. If you talk to her, tell her I hope she feels better soon."

Rather than let her aunt know what she suspected, Emily simply said, "I'll tell her if I talk to her."

Emily called all the numbers she had and left messages for Jillian to call Dr. Blake. No one had seen or heard from Jillian. After Emily hung up from the last number she called, she turned to Kingston.

"Looks like this is turning into a real mystery."

The dog sat up, tilted his head, and let out a soft, "Mmff."

In spite of the situation, Emily couldn't help but laugh. No doubt Kingston could hold his own if trouble came at him, but he sure was a sweet, comical creature—and excellent company.

When the bell on the door jingled, Emily expectantly looked up, hoping it was Jillian. But it wasn't. It was Aunt Sherry, holding a box.

"This is heavy," her aunt said as she carried it toward the counter, where she plopped it with a gentle thud. "I promised Noah he could have some leftovers, and here they are."

"He'll appreciate that." Emily got up, put the leftovers in the fridge, and grabbed a chair to pull it closer to her own. "Do you have time to chat?"

"No, not today. I'm heading over to the hospital to see one of the people in my small group from church." She backed toward the door. "Oh, before I forget—I put a can of disinfectant spray in the box so you can clean your work area. I figured that since you and Jillian share the computer, it might be a good idea. I read somewhere about how many germs are on keyboards."

Emily smiled at her thoughtful aunt. "Thanks, I'll do that."

After Aunt Sherry left, Emily rummaged through the box and found the spray. She figured she might as well clean, since she still had nervous energy after doing everything she could to find Jillian. Besides, like her aunt said, there was something going around.

Noah finally returned a little after five, looking dejected. "No one has seen her since Thursday night, except us when she came in on Friday." He glanced around the office then blinked when his gaze settled on the box from Aunt Sherry. "What's that?"

"Leftovers from my aunt. I just pulled them back out of the refrigerator so you wouldn't forget to take them home."

He laughed. "Thank her for me. I certainly appreciate being fed by one of the best cooks in the county."

"I'll tell her you said that." She hesitated before asking, "Do you think we should call the police about Jillian?"

"Probably," he replied. "I would have thought her mother might do that, but when I asked her, she acted like it was no big deal. That surprised me."

"I've been thinking. . . ," Emily began. "Remember that phone call she said was a wrong number?"

Noah's forehead crinkled as he thought about it. He nodded. "Yes, as a matter of fact, I do remember. Why?"

"If it really had been a wrong number, I don't think she would have spent more than a couple of seconds confirming it. From what I remember, she was on longer than that."

"Have you deleted anything from caller ID since then?" he asked.

"No, I didn't think about that."

Noah came around behind the counter and started scrolling through the numbers until they came to the date and time the allegedly wrong number had come through. He grabbed a slip of paper and jotted down the number. "I don't know if this will get us any closer to Jillian, but it's worth a try. I sure hope she's okay."

Emily offered a sympathetic smile. His compassion never stopped.

"Want me to call?" she offered.

"No, it's probably nothing. I'll call and see if someone needed veterinary care. I think playing dumb is probably the way to handle this."

"Oh, I can play as dumb as the next person," Emily said with a chuckle.

"Not as well as me, I'm afraid."

Emily sat and waited as Noah placed the call. The first thing he did was introduce himself, then he was obviously cut off. He barely had half of his next sentence spoken when he reared back, and his eyebrows shot up. Then he blinked and shook his head as he held the phone out.

"What happened?" she asked.

Noah put the phone back on the cradle. "I just got told to mind my own business and never to call back."

"That's rude."

"Not only is it rude, but it worries me. Since we don't have anything else to go on, I think I need to call this number in to Dwayne and have the sheriff's office check into it." Noah fumbled with some papers and pulled out the police report from the break-in. "We need to pray that they can get to the bottom of this and find Jillian."

He closed his eyes for a moment, so Emily shut hers and said a silent prayer. When she opened them and caught him staring at her, he blinked and cleared his throat.

"I bet Jillian is fine, Noah. She's young. I bet she just decided to take a vacation at the last minute."

Noah pursed his lips and shook his head. "It's still not like her to do this. She knows I'll give her some time off if she needs it."

Emily didn't know what else to say. Something was definitely wrong, and it looked more and more like Jillian's disappearance was somehow related to the break-in. She couldn't imagine how, and she certainly hoped that wasn't the case.

After Noah called Dwayne and gave him the information, he picked up the box of food and asked her to lock up behind them. "There's nothing else we can do now, and it's getting late. I bet you're exhausted after working here all day."

"I'm fine," she replied, although she felt like a bulldozer had run over her.

"Would you like to take Kingston home with you?" he asked. "Mel already said it's okay with him and Sherry."

She nodded. "Sure. Kingston and I get along great."

At the sound of his name, the dog looked up at Emily and panted. She patted him on the head.

They walked out to the parking lot on the side of the strip mall, and Noah put the box inside the cab of his truck before turning back to face Emily. "I appreciate everything you're doing."

She smiled back at him. "I know you do, which makes me want to do more."

For a few seconds they stood there staring at each other, silence interrupted only by the humming sound of insects in the nearby wooded area behind the clinic. Even Kingston remained quiet. Emily was transfixed by the unspoken message between them—a chemistry she could no longer deny, no matter how much she tried.

"Emily." His voice cracked, so he lifted his hand to his mouth and cleared his throat.

She took a step back and turned slightly. "I really need to leave now."

"Tell your aunt I said thanks for the food."

Emily turned, smiled, held the door for Kingston, then got into her car. She didn't trust herself to speak, so she just waved.

❧

Noah felt as though he was swirling in a cyclone of feelings and events that were out of his control. So much had happened in such a short time. The flood had sent everyone scurrying around, trying to find a way to protect their animals. Emily had arrived and quickly filled his mind with thoughts of confused joy. His clinic had been broken into—obviously for the narcotics that he kept double locked. And now Jillian was missing.

He didn't want to expose what he knew about her past, but

if she didn't show up soon, he'd be forced to let the authorities know that Jillian hadn't been to work since the break-in. The last thing he needed to do was impede their investigation. Before this, there was no indication that Jillian had fallen back into her old ways, but there was always that possibility, which was why he'd added another lock to the controlled drug cabinet at the clinic and had it connected to an alarm.

After Noah got to his apartment and put the food away, he jumped into the shower. He'd barely dried off when the phone rang. He contemplated not answering it, but he couldn't resist.

It was Dwayne calling to let him know they'd found Jillian. Noah let out a whistle of relief.

"Good. Now maybe we can get back to normal around the office."

"I don't think so," Dwayne said. "We have her locked up."

"Wha—"

"Can't say right now, but she's asking for you."

Noah didn't hesitate. "I'll be right there."

"I haven't known you all that long, Noah, but I think I know you well enough to give you some advice. This is a troubled young woman, and you took a chance hiring her."

"Yes, I realize that, but I think she's a good girl who got in with the wrong crowd."

Dwayne made a sniffing noise. "Yeah, I can see why you feel that way. Ever think she might be *part* of the wrong crowd?"

Noah understood why Dwayne said that, but he refused to give up on any injured creature—especially a person who had so much potential. "We don't need to talk on the phone right now, Dwayne. I'll be there in a few minutes."

"Gotcha. See ya."

The walls seemed to be closing in around Noah as he sat down on the edge of his bed. He lowered his head, stared at the floor before shutting his eyes, and prayed. He wanted

Jillian to understand that God loved her, in spite of her past. And He loved her now, even though she'd fallen. Or at least it appeared she'd fallen. Sometimes things weren't as they seemed. Noah had enough life experience to know this.

He arrived at the small jail, and Dwayne led him back to a room. "Her court-appointed attorney will be here any minute, so you don't have long."

"Okay, I just wanted to let her know I care enough to come down here."

Dwayne cast a pitying glance his way then shook his head and mumbled something as he walked down the hall to get Jillian. Noah liked the deputy, and he understood why the man was so cynical.

When Jillian walked into the room, she looked about ten years older than she was. Her hair hung in strings around her face, and her clothes looked like she'd slept in them for days. Maybe she had.

"What happened, Jillian?" he asked as he leaned forward.

She looked him in the eye for a split second then looked down. "I don't know."

"You were doing so well. You never gave me any reason not to trust you."

"I know. It's just that. . ." Her voice trailed off, and she let out a tiny whimper.

Noah wanted to assure her that she wasn't in this situation alone. He'd been around her enough to know she was a good person deep down. "I'm praying for you. And I want you to know that when you get out, you can have your job back."

She glanced up at him and glared, an uncharacteristic frown contorting her face. "Why? I don't want people feeling sorry for me."

"I don't feel sorry for you, Jillian," he said firmly. "I just happen to be someone who believes in a smart, personable woman who used to have some friends who are very bad for her."

"How do you know all this?"

He smiled. "Just a good guess."

They sat in silence for a few more seconds before she buried her face in her hands and started crying. "I told him to leave me alone, but he wouldn't. When he called me and said he just wanted to see me to say good-bye, I really thought that's what he wanted."

"Are you talking about your old boyfriend who got you into the mess last year?"

Jillian nodded. "He called me at the clinic and asked me to meet him. I told him that would be the last time, and he said fine because he was leaving town." She blinked back another tear. "Then after we started talking, he told me I was worthless and no one would want me—and no amount of college will make me any better than I am."

"That's not true, and you know it."

She tightened her lips, and her chin began to quiver. Noah reached over and pulled a tissue out of the box on the table. "Where is he?"

"He's in jail, too. After we left the clinic—yeah, I let him in, but he couldn't get the drug cabinet open. Those locks are strong."

"You knew the locks were there, right?"

"Yeah, I've seen you double-check them enough. I was counting on them keeping him out of the cabinet."

Noah nodded. "So what happened after you left the clinic?"

"We went to another friend's place. They'd just scored some stuff from the emergency room at the hospital."

"I won't even ask how," Noah said. "So where did the police pick you up?"

"They found us at his mother's house."

That must have been the woman Noah had spoken to—the one who hung up when he'd asked about Jillian. "What does she have to do with all this?"

Jillian shuddered. "That woman is evil. She took off after you called."

"So you knew about my call, huh?"

A tap came at the door, and Noah stood up. "I won't give up on you, Jillian. I want you to know that we'll be praying for you."

"Is Emily going to keep working for you?"

Noah nodded. "Yes, and I'm going to ask her to work full-time until you get out. Take care, Jillian."

He was all the way to the door before he heard her soft "Good-bye, Noah. I'm really sorry I messed up." Her voice cracked as she added, "Tell Emily—you can tell her everything, and tell her I'm sorry."

Noah didn't look back at her. He focused straight ahead as he left the station and headed toward his apartment. Although he didn't have a bit of an appetite, he fixed a small plate with some of Sherry's leftovers. He needed to keep up his strength.

~

Emily got to work early the next morning, hoping that there would be some development in finding Jillian. Noah hadn't arrived yet, so she got Kingston's bed ready, turned on the computer, and set up the front desk for the day.

She loved being there in the mornings, but working all day made it difficult to do what she came here for—to find herself. The best therapy for Emily was working outdoors, helping Aunt Sherry with her garden and Uncle Mel with the animals. She'd discuss it with Noah and let him know she couldn't continue working full-time for more than a few days.

Noah walked in a half hour later, bags under his eyes, his shoulders sloping downward. When he looked at her, she melted. Then he looked away and continued toward the examining area. It was unlike Noah to walk by without greeting her, so she panicked and jumped up from her chair.

"What's wrong, Noah?"

He stopped and turned to face her. "Jillian's in jail."

"She's what?"

Noah took a deep breath and slowly let it out. "There's some stuff I haven't told you about Jillian, but since all this has happened, I guess you ought to know."

"Yeah." She planted her hands on her hips and glared at him.

"Check when the first appointment is coming in. This'll take awhile."

She looked on the computer and saw that the first appointment wasn't due for almost an hour. "Is that enough time?" she asked.

"Yes, that should be enough time."

He pulled a chair from the waiting area to the reception desk then unfolded the whole story about how Jillian had been caught up with the wrong crowd after high school and gotten into some trouble. Pastor Chuck had counseled her and encouraged her to go to college. Then he asked Noah to hire her part-time. Everything was going smoothly, so there didn't seem to be any reason to talk about her past.

Emily listened to every word Noah said as she sat there stunned. "I had no idea about any of this, Noah. Jillian seems like such a sweet girl."

"I know. And she is when she's not with that loser ex-boyfriend of hers. She also asked me to tell you she's sorry."

Noah obviously wanted to save the world, but Emily felt the same way. Jillian had a tremendous amount of potential. She was smart, wonderful with customers, and she loved animals. In Emily's book, that made her pretty special.

"I'm going to do whatever I can to help her," Noah said. "In the meantime, would you consider working full-time? That is, until Jillian can come back?"

"How long do you think it'll be?" she asked.

Noah shrugged. "Who knows? The court system can be slow, or she could be back in a couple of weeks."

Emily glanced down at the floor as she thought about the conversation she'd planned to have with him. On the one hand, she was justified in telling him she couldn't do it.

However, she liked Jillian, Noah really needed her, and she didn't have anywhere else to be. So how could she turn him down?

"I guess I can for a little while," she replied. "How about you, Kingston? Are you okay with that?"

He looked up at her and expressed his approval. "Mmff."

When Noah smiled at her, the skin around his eyes crinkled. The accompanying flutter in her chest caught her off guard.

"Thank you, Emily. I owe you one." Noah got up and replaced the chair where it belonged. "I have some prep work to do, so just let me know when the first appointment arrives."

The bell sounded, so Emily glanced up, fully expecting a standard-size poodle and its owner, but instead, Aunt Sherry came bounding through the door, grinning from ear to ear. "I have a surprise for you and Noah! Where is he?"

seven

"He's prepping for a patient," Emily said. "Whatcha got?"

Aunt Sherry grinned. "Just something I know both of you like."

"You're not gonna tell me, are you?"

"Nope." Her aunt patted her oversized tote. "It's right here. I'll sit in this chair and wait until Noah's finished with whatever he's doing."

"That might be a while. His patient should be here any minute." A big white SUV pulled into the space out front. "In fact, here he is right now."

Within a minute, Seymour the poodle and his exuberant owner came walking in. Kingston got up and walked around to see who'd just entered. Emily pointed to the floor beside her. "Sit." Kingston sat.

"Wait right here, Seymour," the woman said to her dog. "I have to check you in."

"Hi, Mrs. Whitley." Emily grinned at the woman then turned to Seymour. "Hey, Seymour. Ready to see Dr. Blake?"

The poodle got excited at the sound of his name, so he forgot his order and came around the counter. Emily held her breath for a moment before she realized Kingston wasn't about to disobey her, no matter what Seymour did.

Emily had been warned about Mrs. Whitley's dog who'd been through a couple of obedience classes but still couldn't control his urges. All the pampering his owner gave him spoiled the dog and made him a pest around other animals.

The two dogs sniffed each other, but the Great Dane remained planted in his spot. After a few seconds of not getting a reaction, Seymour lost interest and headed back to his master. However, he suddenly stopped, sniffed the air, and instantly bounded toward Aunt Sherry, whose eyes widened at the surprise.

"No-no, Seymour, honey," Mrs. Whitley said in the voice she obviously reserved for her precious poodle.

Seymour wasn't listening. He knew Aunt Sherry had something good in her tote, and with one sweeping swipe of the paw, he'd knocked her tote off the chair next to her. Suddenly there was a mad scramble for the bag.

"No, Seymour!" Aunt Sherry hollered. "Down!"

The poodle jumped back at the sound of her harsh tone, but that didn't stop him from diving back toward the bag a second later. By now Emily had no doubt Seymour wouldn't stop until he got whatever he wanted, so she went around to the waiting area with the leash she kept beside her. She counted on him remembering some of the commands from obedience training.

"Sit, Seymour," Emily said. The second he obeyed the command, she snapped the leash on his collar before he had a chance to think about what was in Aunt Sherry's bag. "Come on, boy, I have a treat for you."

"Oh, he can't have a treat," Mrs. Whitley said. "I have him on a very special diet."

Emily cast a glance at Aunt Sherry, who still looked shell-shocked, and turned back to face the dog's owner. "He's going to get a treat, whether I give him one or he gets it from her bag. It's just a little piece of dog food anyway, so don't worry."

Mrs. Whitley swallowed hard and looked over at Aunt Sherry. "I—I guess it's okay if he has a treat at the doctor's office."

Noah chose that moment to come out for the dog. "Hey, Mrs. Whitley, how's Seymour?"

The poodle forgot all about the treat, jumped toward Noah before Emily snapped the leash, and the dog landed on his rear. He let out a whimper, but Noah didn't let him get too distressed before taking the leash from Emily. "I've got him." He squatted down next to Seymour. "How's my big buddy?"

Seymour licked him across the face in response.

Noah wiped his face with his sleeve and grinned at Mrs. Whitley. "He looks healthy. How's the obedience training coming along?"

His poor owner looked frazzled as she shook her head. "Not so well, I'm afraid. I still can't make him behave."

"You just have to stick with it. He's still young. His attention span will grow as he gets older."

Emily thought about the Great Dane who remained behind the counter. She could only imagine how curious he must have been, yet he was so well trained he didn't budge.

"Perhaps you should consider going through the training with him," Noah advised. "Sometimes all it takes is for him to see that you mean business. They can teach you how to be firm."

The woman flipped her hand at the wrist. "Oh, I couldn't do that. I'd hate to break his spirit."

Emily and her aunt exchanged a knowing glance. She'd seen plenty of disobedient animals, and almost every one of them would have been easy to train if their owners had been willing to spend more time working with them.

Noah tugged on Seymour's leash. "C'mon, boy, let's go see how you're doing." He cast a look over to Mrs. Whitley. "Would you like to join us?"

She scrunched her face. "I can't bear watching him get his shots."

"Then you better stay out here. We won't be long."

Emily and her aunt chatted with Mrs. Whitley until Seymour was finished with his checkup and shots. As soon as Noah opened the door from the examining area, the proud poodle pranced out into the waiting room like he owned the place. Kingston whimpered, but after a stern glance from Emily, he remained in his spot.

Noah found himself continuing to lose his heart to Emily, a piece at a time. As he watched her handle each situation that came her way, he knew she could do anything she set her mind to. Not only was she organized, friendly, and professional, she had a knack with animals and for putting people at ease.

After Seymour and Mrs. Whitley left, Sherry carried her tote across the room and hoisted it onto the reception counter. "I brought you some sustenance," she announced with pride. "Emily's favorite blueberry oatmeal muffins." He watched her pull out a plastic bag filled to capacity with treats he knew would be tasty. When she opened the bag, a delicious aroma filled the clinic.

"You didn't have to do that, Aunt Sherry." Emily's cheeks were pink, and she wouldn't look him in the eye.

"Oh, but I'm glad she did." Noah reached into the bag and pulled out a muffin. One taste and he felt like he was floating on clouds. "This is absolutely delicious."

Sherry fastened her tote and grinned. "I'm glad you like it." She edged toward the door and waved. "I know you're busy, so I'll leave the two of you to your work." Then she winked at Emily. "See you when you get home, sugar."

As soon as the door closed behind her, Noah looked at her and smiled. "Sherry is amazing. You're fortunate to have her."

"Yes, I know." Emily still didn't look him in the eye, so he turned back toward the examining rooms. "I need to clean up then call on a couple of farms before my afternoon appointments."

He took his time cleaning since he wasn't expected at the first farm for another hour. For once he wasn't slammed. He would have loved to spend a little time with Emily, but since she seemed flustered and unsure this morning, he figured it might be better to leave her alone until she worked through whatever was bothering her.

Soon it was time for him to leave. "These are short visits,

so I'll see you in a couple of hours."

Emily glanced up, then her gaze quickly darted to something on the floor. He glanced down and spotted a fifty-dollar bill beside his feet, so he picked it up. "Any idea whose this is?"

She nodded. "It has to be Mrs. Whitley's."

"Are you sure it doesn't belong to your aunt?"

"I'm pretty sure it wouldn't be my aunt's because she was sitting over there." Emily pointed to another row of chairs. "Besides, she's not likely to walk around with a fifty."

On top of everything else, she had to be the most honest woman he'd ever met. "Why don't you call Mrs. Whitley and ask if she wants us to send her a check or if she'd rather pick up the money next time she's out."

"I'll do that right now."

Noah walked out of the clinic, headed to his truck, and tossed a few things into the back before getting in. Emily's image played in his mind as he drove to the first farm.

He knew it wasn't right to compare, but he couldn't help holding her next to Tiffany in his mind. If Tiffany had seen the fifty-dollar bill, he wasn't sure she would have mentioned it to him. Instead, she would have considered the finders-keepers rule and spent the money on herself.

There were too many differences between the two women to count. What he saw in Tiffany back a few years ago was now a mystery to Noah. Sure she was pretty, but lots of girls were. She was smart, but her goal in life was to marry well and have her days free to hang out at the country club and get her nails done. Not that he expected her to be a career woman, but he at least wished she had some purpose outside her own personal circle that seemed to get smaller as time went on.

When Noah arrived at the first farm, all he had to do was check a couple of the goats and administer medication to a horse with an infected foot. He was back in his truck less than an hour later.

His second stop was even shorter. A year earlier this farmer had to sell off some of his land to pay his taxes, so Noah didn't expect to see the payment for his services—at least not any time soon.

As he got back in the truck, his thoughts drifted to the business side of his practice. He made enough to survive and pay the bills on the clinic. However, what he considered a decent income would have been debatable with his father, whose practice had flourished over the years simply because his clientele was more upscale than any of the ones Noah served.

There were times when Noah thought about calling his delinquent clients to see if they could arrange a payment plan, but the staggering amount some of them owed might freak them out. Most of the people who brought smaller animals into the clinic paid as they went, but he billed the farmers. When he had time, he actually mailed the bills. Lately he'd been so busy he'd let it slip. In fact, he couldn't remember the last billing he'd mailed. He'd intended to get Jillian on that project soon, but he hadn't even had time for that.

№

Emily finished all the daily work and started looking around for something else to do. When she was sure she'd covered everything Noah had asked her to do, she pulled her sketch pad from her tote and doodled.

After a few minutes she felt guilty because she was on Noah's clock, so she put down the sketch pad and clicked through the files on the computer to see if any loose ends needed to be tied up.

When she got to the Blalock farm account, she stopped and stared at the screen, stunned by what she saw. The farmer owed Noah more than a thousand dollars, and he hadn't even shown an attempt to pay a dime of it.

This prompted her to check all the other farm accounts, and she quickly saw that the Blalock account was the norm, not the exception. After clicking through every account in the Noah's Ark system, she realized that the only people who paid were customers who brought their patients into the clinic and a very small handful of farmers, including her aunt and uncle.

She jotted down some of the larger accounts and came up with a staggering total. If everyone paid what they owed, Noah would be able to hire a full office staff and never have to bat an eye.

Emily knew this was a ministry of sorts for Noah, but it was also his livelihood. He wouldn't be able to stay in business if he didn't collect some of the money he was owed. She'd have to figure out a way to talk to him without sounding like she was nosing into his business.

The phone rang, and it was Noah. "I'm stopping off at a deli on my way back. What are you in the mood for?"

"Turkey on wheat with lettuce and tomato," she replied. "I'll pay you when you get here."

He laughed. "That's not necessary. You're doing so much for me, I wouldn't even think about asking for money from you."

"We'll discuss that later," she said.

After they got off the phone, she brainstormed ways to collect some of the money Noah was owed. No matter what she came up with, she knew he'd balk, but she couldn't just sit back and do nothing. He obviously made enough money to stay in business, but she knew he had so much more potential if he collected what was owed.

Noah arrived a half hour later. "Here's the food. I need to put this stuff away and wash up. You don't have to wait for me."

"That's okay," she mumbled. "I'll wait."

They could discuss the billing issue after lunch, since there wasn't anything on the schedule for another hour. Emily dreaded bringing it up because she had no idea what Noah's reaction would be. One thing she was fairly certain of, though, was that he wouldn't even consider strong-arm tactics. And that was one of the things she found most attractive about him.

Noah was a strong man with a gentle spirit. His generosity was a major bonus but also his biggest flaw. A giving nature was an admirable trait, but he didn't know when to stop.

At the sound of Noah's footsteps drawing closer, Emily shoved her scratch paper into the pencil drawer. He opened the bag, pulled out a wrapped sandwich, and handed it to her. "I got both of us the same thing," he said. "I got chips, too, but I had no idea what kind you liked, so I got a bag of each."

Emily laughed. "You don't have to do that, Noah."

He put his sandwich down and let his gaze settle on her. "I know I don't have to, but I want to. No amount of money can repay you for all you're doing for me and this clinic."

She let out a nervous chuckle. "You're paying me for my time here, and it's all part of my job."

"It's more than that." Noah broke his gaze and reached for the sandwich. As he slowly unwrapped it, Emily could tell by the set of his jaw that his mind was somewhere else.

Emily took a bite of her sandwich and let silence prevail. She'd been around Noah enough to know he didn't always have to have conversation filling every moment.

After she swallowed her second bite, she put down her sandwich. "So how was the Jenkins clan?"

Noah shook his head as he finished chewing. "I feel so bad for Patrick Jenkins. After he sold that last piece of land, his heart doesn't seem to be in his farming anymore."

Emily had already heard about the hard times that had fallen on many of her aunt and uncle's friends and fellow farmers. "Maybe things will turn around." This definitely wasn't the time to bring up billing.

The phone rang, and this time it was Jillian. "Want to talk to Noah?" Emily asked.

"No."

Her answer was so abrupt Emily was startled. "Okay, so what's going on?"

"Can you come to my mom's place after work? I need to

talk to someone, and I'm not allowed to go anywhere."

"Um. . ." Emily glanced at Noah, who sat there watching, waiting. "I guess so. Want me to bring you anything?"

Jillian coughed. "Just a listening ear and the willingness to believe me."

"I can do that," Emily promised. "Now I need your mother's address."

After Emily hung up, Noah cocked his head and stared at her. "Well?"

Her throat tightened. "That was Jillian. She asked me to come over after work."

"I'll go with you."

Emily glanced down then looked Noah squarely in the eye. "She wants me to come alone."

The look of concern on his face touched Emily. "I don't want to put you in jeopardy," he said.

She smiled. "I'll be fine."

"Call me the second you leave so I won't worry."

eight

Emily hadn't even sat down before Jillian blurted out, "I don't deserve to live after what I did."

"What, exactly, did you do?"

She and Jillian were now at the kitchen table in her mother's tiny cottage. Emily couldn't help but notice the peeling paint and timeworn furniture.

Jillian folded her hands and stared at them for what seemed like an eternity before she looked Emily in the eye. "Did Noah tell you anything about my past?"

Emily nodded.

"When Brad told me he wanted to stop off at the clinic, I told him no because it was closed."

"After all the things I heard about him, why would you even be with him?" Emily asked.

The younger woman shrugged. "Just lonely, I guess. Mom comes and goes, and I haven't made friends with anyone at school. The few people I knew in high school moved away."

Emily reached for Jillian's hand. "I'm your friend. And Noah really cares about you."

"Yes, I know he does. That's why I feel so awful."

This Brad guy must have something Jillian needed. "You're a very smart woman, Jillian. Why do you let Brad do this to you?"

Jillian blinked but not in time to stop a tear that trickled down her cheek. "He told me he loved me and that he'd do anything to make me happy." She sniffled. "And I've been so sad lately it sounded good."

"I didn't realize you were sad," Emily said. "And I don't think Noah knew either."

"There was no point in burdening you and Noah with my feelings. I figured both of you had enough on your minds."

Emily smiled and squeezed Jillian's hand. "So tell me why he said he wanted to go to the clinic."

Jillian pursed her lips and shuddered. "It's really stupid."

"That's okay. Tell me anyway." Emily squeezed her hand.

Jillian sucked in a deep breath and slowly blew it out. "His cat eats this expensive food, and Brad was broke, and we carry it at the clinic. I told him we didn't sell much of it, so he convinced me it would be good to go get some since it would go bad anyway, and he'd write a check after he got paid."

Emily could tell how heartbroken Jillian was, so she refrained from asking again why she'd trust Brad. "Why didn't you call Noah when you realized what Brad was really there for—or at any time? He could have stopped Brad from getting you into trouble."

"I—I couldn't. Noah's the last person I'd want to upset. I begged Brad to get out of there, but he just laughed at me." She pulled her hand away from Emily's and held it out. "Now I've completely blown any chance of having Noah's trust."

"It's not that he doesn't trust you, Jillian. I think we're both concerned about your judgment at this very difficult time in your life."

Jillian shook her head. "No one can understand what it feels like to be in my shoes. I never knew my father, and my mother only wants me around when she needs something."

"You're right," Emily replied. She pondered how much she should say before finally deciding it was best to come out with it. Even if it hurt to talk about it, she might be able to relate to Jillian on her level. "I don't know what it feels like to be in your shoes, but I do know what it feels like to have a mother who doesn't want you."

Jillian snorted. "How would you know?"

"My own mother abandoned me at one of the worst times

of my life. I spent all of my teenage years wondering what I'd done wrong."

The younger woman's eyes widened. "What did you do? Where did you go?"

Emily closed her eyes and said a silent prayer for guidance. "Fortunately for me, my father was still there. He did the best he could, but there were times he was clueless."

"At least you had someone."

"Yes," she admitted. "I also had Aunt Sherry and Uncle Mel who have given me unconditional love all my life. There was never any doubt I had someone who cared."

"I don't—well, besides Noah—and you."

"There's someone else," Emily said softly. "I know you've spoken to Pastor Chuck about this, and I don't want to preach at you."

Jillian bobbed her head. "Yeah, we've talked several times, and he keeps talking about how much Jesus loves me. But where was He when my mother told me I was good for nothing?"

"He's right there with you all the time," Emily replied. "I don't have all the answers about why things like this happen, but remember that you never have to walk alone in life. Just understand that sometimes people you care about will disappoint you."

With a half smile, Jillian nodded. "Yeah, like I disappointed Noah."

Emily leaned back in her chair. "Noah will trust you again someday. It'll take time, but believe me, he's a forgiving man."

"I know he is."

"Good. Now tell me what's going on with your court date."

They discussed when she had to report to court. "I'd like to come back to work for Noah after this is all over—that is, if he'll have me." She grew pensive as she flicked a bread crumb off the table. "But I'll understand if he won't."

"I'm not a hundred percent sure what he'll do, but I bet

he'll give you another chance." Emily paused until she caught Jillian's gaze. "Especially if you promise not to see Brad again."

Jillian opened her mouth then closed it without uttering a sound. Emily realized how difficult this was for Jillian, but ultimately she was responsible for her own actions. After all, she was an adult. Too bad she didn't have the coping skills she needed.

"Is there anything you'd like for me to tell Noah?" Emily asked as she stood up to leave.

"Tell him I'm really sorry and that I'll do anything to make it up to him."

Suddenly an idea popped into Emily's head. "Why don't you start going to church with us? You know Pastor Chuck. He preaches great sermons."

"I know. I heard one once on a CD he gave me." She followed Emily to the door. "But I'm not sure I'm ready to go to church. Let me think about it."

"Just remember that you don't have to be ready. Jesus will accept you as you are."

Jillian nodded then smiled. "So how are things between you and Noah?"

"Huh?"

"I've seen the way you two look at each other. There are definitely sparks."

Was she that obvious? Emily didn't want to take any chances on people jumping to conclusions just because she was so easy to read, so she shook her head. "Noah and I have a lot of respect for each other. That's all."

"Right," Jillian said with a smirk.

"I'll call you about church, okay?" Emily had reached the front porch, so she turned around to wait for an answer.

With a slight hesitation, Jillian nodded. "Fine."

After she gave Jillian a hug, Emily headed out to her car. All the way home she rehashed her conversation with the hurting young woman. She remembered wondering where God was when her mother left. How could He have put her through something like that when she needed her mother the most? She'd searched scripture, trying to figure out what the whole Christianity thing was all about. The magnitude of what people endured in biblical times made her feel that her problems were small next to some of theirs. However, it still hadn't made her pain go away. Now that she was an adult, she understood that God hadn't made it happen, but He'd used the bad situation to help her grow as a Christian.

Then there was the issue of her feelings for Noah. Yes, she did have what she used to call a crush on him, but wouldn't anyone in her shoes? After all, he was a smart, sweet man with a heart for Christ that spilled over into everything else he did.

Emily slowed down as she drove past the clinic on the way home, and she noticed that the lights were still on. Noah worked such long hours, it was amazing he had any energy left.

She was tempted to stop and give him a full report about her meeting with Jillian, but she decided not to. That could wait until tomorrow. It was time to go home and see what she could do to help Uncle Mel and Aunt Sherry. They'd been awesome about everything.

As soon as she walked into the kitchen, Aunt Sherry pointed to the hallway. "Why don't you kick off your shoes and take a rest? Dinner will be ready in about half an hour."

"I want to help."

"No need. I threw a bunch of stuff in a casserole dish and made a salad before I left to run errands this morning. All I had to do was stick the dish in the oven, and I'll toss the salad right before we eat."

"Then I'll go back outside and see if Uncle Mel can use some help."

Aunt Sherry gave her a puzzled look. "Was he out there when you got home?"

"No, I didn't see him. Why?"

"He probably isn't back yet, then. He finished all his chores and headed into town to meet with a bunch of men from the church. They're banding together to help some of the farmers who aren't as fortunate as us."

Emily smiled. One of the things she loved about farm life here in West Virginia was how everyone worked together for the good of all.

When Uncle Mel got home, they sat down to eat. Aunt Sherry asked him one question after another, but Emily only heard a fraction of his answers. She'd drifted into a world of her own thoughts when she realized it had suddenly grown quiet and that her aunt and uncle were staring at her.

She cast a sheepish glance down then forced a smile as she looked back up. "Sorry, but today has been kind of insane."

Uncle Mel stretched both arms over the table and nodded. "I heard. Wanna talk about it?"

"What did you hear?" Emily hadn't said a word about her conversation with Jillian to anyone.

"Well," he began slowly, "I know about Noah's assistant being involved in the break-in and that you went to visit her after work."

Aunt Sherry obviously knew, too, because she didn't look the least bit surprised. "Did she explain why she did it?"

"Sort of." Emily wasn't sure how much to tell or if she should keep everything to herself.

"Did she ask you not to discuss it with anyone?"

Emily shook her head. "No, not really. It's just that— well. . ."

"That's okay," Aunt Sherry said. "You don't have to tell us. We can still pray for her. I do know enough about the girl to know she can use all the prayers we can give."

"Ain't that the truth," Uncle Mel agreed. He looked at his wife. "Did you fix dessert?"

"No, I did something better. When I stopped off at the

bakery this morning, I picked up a dozen of your favorite peanut butter cookies."

The grin on Uncle Mel's face said it all. He definitely approved.

After Emily helped Aunt Sherry clean the kitchen, she headed to her room and pulled out her cell phone to see if she had any messages. There were three—one from Jillian and two from Noah. She called Jillian first.

"Hey, look, Emily, I've been thinking. . ."

When she didn't speak for a few seconds, Emily urged her. "About what?"

"You said God was with me all the time. I have some questions about that."

"Would you like for me to come over tomorrow during lunch? We can talk about it then."

"Do you mind?" Jillian's voice squeaked with uncertainty.

"Of course I don't mind. There's nothing I love talking about more than the Lord. He's walked with me for as long as I can remember. Without Him, I wouldn't be here today."

Next Emily called Noah. "Hey, I wondered how your visit with Jillian went."

"It was good. She told me what happened."

"You do believe her, don't you?" Noah asked.

"Yes, I do. Have you spoken with her?"

Noah hesitated for a couple of seconds before speaking. "I have."

"That's good. Did she tell you what all she and I talked about?"

"She said you mentioned something about going to church on Sunday. I told her that was an excellent idea. I'll see if I can get permission from the court for her to leave the house."

"Oh, I didn't think about that," Emily admitted. "But now I understand why she called a little while ago. I guess she just needed that little extra encouragement you gave her."

"That's not a bad thing. We all need encouragement."

The way he said that made Emily feel like he'd left something unsaid. "I'll be in early in the morning because I told Jillian I'd come over to her place for lunch. There's something I'd like to discuss with you."

"You're not leaving us, are you?"

"Leaving? No, of course not. It has nothing to do with me." A nervous chuckle escaped his lips. "Sorry, I'm not being paranoid or anything. It's just that I like having you at the clinic. You have such a calming effect on my clients."

Emily laughed. "I'm glad I'm good for something."

༄

The next morning Noah arrived about five minutes before Emily. When she pulled up, his pulse quickened, but he managed to hide his excitement when she walked in. His feelings for her had advanced beyond the professional stage, and he didn't want to let her know—at least not yet. Not until he had some idea of how she felt about him. "Have a seat. I'll get you some coffee."

"You don't have to wait on me, Noah. I can get my own coffee."

He picked up his mug, went around behind the counter, and sat down in the extra chair he'd brought back there. Emily joined him in less than a minute, a steaming cup of coffee in one fist and a couple of bagels in the other. "Aunt Sherry sent these, so I brought you one."

"So what was so important that you needed to come in early?"

The strain on Emily's face was apparent as she braced herself to break some news. That made him nervous, but he'd learned to take deep breaths and loosen his jaw.

"I noticed that some of your clients have owed you money since you've been here," she blurted as her face turned bright crimson. "And they haven't even made an attempt to pay."

"Yeah, that's true. I'm not sure what I can do about it though." He studied her face and watched her expression change.

"You can't let people take advantage of you, Noah. You're such a nice guy, people will run all over you."

Noah had to smile at that. "Trust me, Emily. No one's running all over me. I don't do anything I don't want to do."

She calmed down. "Maybe it's none of my business, but I worked up a plan that might help you get some of that money." When he didn't say anything, she added, "I think most people want to pay their bills, but they only see the full amount, which in some cases is staggering."

He tilted his head to one side. "Oh yeah? So let's say I was interested in some sort of recovery plan. What would we do?"

"Well, first," she said as she held up one finger and touched it with the index finger of her other hand, "we can send a letter reminding people what they owe."

"They get a monthly bill as it is," he said. "I think they know what they owe."

"But this would be different. We could write a letter explaining why you need to collect the money. They can work on a payment plan if they can't afford the entire balance, which I'm sure many of them can't."

"You're right about that," he agreed. He shoved the last of the bagel into his mouth, folded his arms, and stretched out his legs to hear the rest of her plan.

"All they need to pay is a small amount for you to continue rendering services." She slowed down and cast a wary glance toward him at the tail end of that sentence, as if checking to see his reaction.

"So what we're saying, in essence, is that if they don't pay something, they can find another vet?"

She shrugged, held up her hands, and let them fall with a slap onto her jeans-clad thighs. "In a roundabout way, I guess."

"I don't know," he said. "I'll have to think about that one. The thought of an animal needing medical care and not getting it just because of money doesn't sit well with me." He snickered. "I guess I must take after my dad. When he first opened his practice, some of his clients didn't pay on time. That stopped when he hired Hazel, a woman who turned things around for him within a month. His clients could certainly afford his services though. Some of mine might not be able to."

From the look on her face, he knew she understood. She was trying to be pragmatic and help him but not at the risk of his animal patients not getting the care they needed.

"Do you have any other ideas how we can do this?" he asked.

She shook her head. "Not really. But I can draft a letter, and we can discuss it before it goes out."

"Okay, why don't you do that?" he said. "Just don't send it out until I give you the go-ahead."

She smiled and nodded. "Of course."

They talked about Jillian next. He'd already spoken to Dwayne, who offered to help get permission for the girl to go to church, as long as someone trustworthy accompanied her. Noah offered to be that person. Dwayne said he'd be happy to help as well, since someone had done the same thing for him when he was searching.

The phone rang, so Emily stopped to answer it. He could tell it was her aunt as soon as she started talking. She laughed then held the phone out to Noah.

"She wants to talk to you."

He took the phone and answered a few questions. Then Sherry asked him to come to dinner that night and then again Sunday after church. She even said if he had time he could come over on Friday night and Saturday, too. With a chuckle, he said he could probably swing one or two times. After he got off the phone, he told Emily, hoping she'd give some indication of her feelings about him being around so much during her personal time.

"I'm so sorry, Noah. My aunt means well, but I need to talk

to her and let her know it's awkward."

"Awkward? How so?"

"There's nothing but a professional friendship between us. I don't want her putting you on the spot like that."

A sinking feeling flooded Noah. He needed to protect his heart, or he'd be an emotional wreck.

nine

The expression on Noah's face confused Emily. He looked hurt. Had she misread him?

His appearance quickly changed to one of fierce determination. "I can handle it, but if it makes you uncomfortable, please, by all means, talk to her."

She sensed that something between them had shifted. "I will."

He put a few more feet of distance between them then paused. "If you want to draft a letter for my nonpaying clients, you may. I'll take a look at whatever you have and make adjustments if necessary."

Noah left Emily sitting there in silence with nothing but her thoughts rumbling through her head. His tone was sharp and edgy, without the warm friendliness she was accustomed to.

Between patients, Emily worked on a letter, but it didn't come easy. She typed a paragraph and deleted most of it then started over. No matter what she put on the page, it sounded harsh or trite. It was much more difficult than she thought it would be. Maybe she should leave things as they were. After all, this wasn't a permanent job for her. As soon as Jillian got back and she figured out what she wanted to do with her life, she'd be gone.

Emily's stomach knotted at the very thought of moving on. She liked it here. Aunt Sherry and Uncle Mel made her feel like she was home. Their farm felt safe. West Virginia was beautiful. Now that she thought about it, working at Noah's Ark gave her a sense of purpose. This was nothing like what she'd expected when she first arrived.

Okay, now that she had those thoughts behind her, she'd

write a killer letter. She turned back to face the computer and cranked out a letter in half an hour. It would have been done sooner if she hadn't had to answer the phone a dozen times. She typed Noah's name at the end then sat back and read it. Not bad. A few minor tweaks and it came across friendly but firm.

The next time Noah stuck his head out the door to see if his patient had arrived, Emily motioned for him to come and take a look at the letter. She'd printed it and had it on the counter, waiting.

He picked it up and slowly read it before looking up. "Not bad. Would you mind handing me a pen? I want to make a couple of changes, but you did a very nice job."

When he handed the paper back to her, she saw that he'd only changed a couple of insignificant things, but he didn't alter a single major point. She caught him staring at her.

"You did a very nice job, Emily." His voice had softened a little, but it still wasn't back to the same friendly tone he'd had before their talk. "I think this might get some results without insulting anyone."

"Thank you." Emily swallowed hard. "Would you like for me to print it and get it out this week?"

"Sure, if you can. I don't want you stressing over it though."

"It's not stressful."

"Okay, good. Let me know when the next patient arrives."

One of the farmers who'd managed to escape the flood stopped by with a box of kittens. Noah didn't normally board animals, but he kept cages and pens for emergencies.

"I sure hope you can find them good homes," he said. "We already have enough barn cats. Any more and the ones we've got will starve to death."

Emily wasn't sure what to do, so she went back and got Noah, who was lecturing the owner of a very temperamental Doberman puppy that he needed to get control over the dog or he'd regret it. It was hard for Emily to imagine the frisky, friendly little puppy turning out bad, but she'd seen all kinds of dogs who hadn't gotten the training they needed.

Bruiser put his front paws on her as she walked into the room, and he bounced around on his hind legs. She started to reach down and pet him, but when Noah gave her a sign and shook his head, she pulled her hand back.

"Sorry to bother you, Noah," she said, "but there's someone here with a box of kittens."

Noah's shoulders slumped. "Barn kittens?"

Emily nodded. "He says he already has too many cats. What should I tell him?"

"I was just about to finish up here. Why don't you ask if he can wait about five minutes?"

"Okay." Emily headed back to the front, leaving Noah to the rest of his lecture about obedience training.

The farmer had already made himself comfortable in one of the chairs, with the box of mewing kittens at his feet. Emily had to resist the urge to go over and peek inside the box. She was such a pushover for baby animals that she knew she wouldn't be able to keep her emotions in check.

The man with the puppy came out and paid his bill. Noah followed shortly afterward. His face lit up when he saw who the farmer was.

"Hey, Barry! I hear you have some kittens to give away."

"I reckon I do." Farmer Barry picked up the box and set it on the chair. "They're mighty cute little things, but it wouldn't be right to keep 'em."

"You know how I feel about spaying and neutering," Noah said as he looked down into the box then lifted his gaze to the other man's. "I'll give you a discount if you let me take care of all your cats."

The farmer pursed his lips then let his head drop forward. "I know I ought to do that. Maybe after we get this crop in."

"Don't wait too much longer, or you'll have another box of kittens. It's gotten harder to place them since the flooding."

"Yeah, I know. Maybe in a couple of weeks, okay?"

"Sounds good," Noah said.

With that, the farmer left empty-handed. Noah lifted the box, turned to Emily, and shook his head laughing. "I'll take a picture with my digital camera this afternoon, and maybe we can send out a few e-mails to church members."

Another farmer, Mack Pierce, brought in some chickens. "Something's wrong with these hens," he said. "They used to be some of my best layers, and I haven't gotten any eggs from them in a while."

"Why didn't you just call? I could have come out to your farm."

"I know how busy you are, and I had some business in town, so I figured it was just as easy for me to bring 'em here."

"Thanks. I'll take a look at them," Noah assured him. "Can you leave them overnight?"

"Yeah," Mack said as he placed his hand on his hip. "I'll come back first thing tomorrow and pick them up. I hope there's nothing serious."

"Probably not," Noah said. "I'll let you know in the morning."

The animal shelter called with a couple of dogs that needed neutering, and since the regular vet who did that was swamped, Noah agreed to take them. The shelter folks arrived fifteen minutes later and dropped off the dogs.

"I don't think we can take in any more animals, no matter what the circumstances are," Noah informed her. "I sure hope no one else comes or calls with an emergency."

The remainder of the morning was busy enough to keep Emily occupied but not crazy like some days had been. Shortly after noon, Emily went to the back and told Noah she was leaving for lunch at Jillian's.

"Want me to bring you something back?" she asked.

"No thanks. I brought my lunch. Give Jillian my best, and tell her we're all praying for her."

"Okay," she said as she backed out of the room. She started to close the door behind her when she decided to address their discussion earlier. "I don't know what I said to upset you, Noah, but whatever it was, I'm sorry."

The instant she said that, a pained expression popped back onto his face. "Don't worry about it."

❧

After Emily left, Noah sank down on the bench in the examining room. He wanted to kick himself for falling in love with Emily. Any normal guy would have learned his lesson by now and known not to trust his own heart.

Tiffany and Emily couldn't have been any more different. Tiffany's gold-digging mind-set had been obvious to everyone but Noah. After they parted ways, his heart was bruised but not completely broken. However, when Emily eventually moved, he knew she'd break his heart completely. The very thought of not seeing her sent him into a state of depression.

No matter how hard he tried, he couldn't find anything about her that would make him want to go the other way. It was obvious to other people as well. Pastor Chuck had said something about how love makes a man smile more—and that was when Noah was grinning from ear to ear. Sherry and Mel weren't matchmaking without encouragement from him. In fact, he'd given Mel a hint of how he felt about Emily. Mel had warned him that Emily had some abandonment issues to work through. Even her father's death felt like rejection.

Noah knew that Emily had planned her stay to be temporary—that she was there to figure out what to do with the rest of her life. He liked her right where she was—in his office, helping him build his business in the right kind of way, with a Christian attitude. Even her letter showed a gentle, caring spirit.

He ate his lunch alone. Well, maybe not alone but without human companionship. Chickens, dogs, and cats didn't count.

"What are you looking at?" he asked in the direction of the

cage holding one of the eggless chickens. "Haven't you ever seen a man feel sorry for himself before?"

The chicken squawked, and he laughed. He was either losing his mind, or he had it worse than he thought. In Noah's experience, being in love was painful.

❧

Jillian was back to her old self, so lunch was relaxing. They chatted about some of the clinic patients and had a good laugh over the variety of farm animals they saw.

"We have a full house as of this morning," Emily said. "You should see all the critters in that office."

Jillian giggled. "I always get a kick out of the animals that come through the door. Did I ever tell you about the choking snake?"

Emily shuddered. "I love all animals except snakes. They give me the creeps."

"This one was funny. Some guy had gotten a snake and fed him a mouse."

That mental image was disgusting, but Emily didn't want to interrupt her friend. "So what happened?"

"Have you ever watched a snake digest its food?"

Emily shook her head. "No, that's one thing I've never seen."

"You can see the form of the animal as it moves through the snake. The guy was certain his snake was choking because it didn't chew its food well enough."

That made Emily laugh. "I don't know much about snakes, but even I know better than that."

"Noah had to give the guy a talk on the care and feeding of a snake," Jillian said, still laughing. "I think he might have gotten rid of it after realizing he couldn't handle it."

"Do a lot of people bring in snakes?" Emily asked. "That's one creature I'm not fond of."

"No, fortunately that was the only one. I really don't like them much either."

That was a relief. "Right now we have a litter of barn

kittens we need to find homes for. Know anyone who might want one?"

"I might," Jillian replied.

"Who?"

"Me. I have to give up Brad and all my old friends who might get me into more trouble. I'm getting lonelier by the minute. You're the only person who bothers with me."

"Don't forget about Noah."

Jillian smiled. "Yes, and Noah. But I might take one of the kittens. Are they cute?"

Emily nodded. "Yes. Very cute. In fact, I'm thinking about taking one, too. Aunt Sherry is anxious to have a house pet, and I think this might make her happy."

"Would that make us related?" Jillian asked. "Sort of?"

"Yes, I think we can claim a family tie there."

"So what else is going on?"

"We've been super busy," Emily said. "I've been working full-time, and when I leave every day, I'm exhausted."

"I'm really sorry." A sad expression fell over Jillian's face. "I messed things up for everyone."

"We believe in you, Jillian." Emily reached for her friend's hands. "The only advice I can give you is to keep your focus on straightening up your life and don't give Brad a chance to ruin anything. You have way too much going for you."

"You really think so?"

Emily nodded. "I know so. If this hadn't happened, I never would have known you had anything but a perfect past. You impressed me from the very beginning."

Jillian's eyes instantly misted. "Thank you so much for telling me that. I've never had anyone who believed in me before."

"We believe in you. Not only that, we need you." Emily paused for emphasis. "I need you."

"You'd think Noah would at least hire one more person to help him in the back," Jillian said. "But I'm glad you're there in the mornings to help out. I always felt so bad about not being able to get there until the afternoon."

Emily thought about that for a moment. If Jillian had felt so bad leaving the reception area of the clinic unattended in the mornings, she should have thought about the impact of letting her boyfriend into the clinic when it was closed. If it hadn't been for the powerful locks and alarm system Noah had on the controlled-drug cabinet, Jillian would have been in a whole lot more trouble than she was now.

Suddenly Jillian broke into a grin as she clapped her hands together. "I finally have my court date!"

"Good." Emily leaned forward and gave Jillian a hug. "How long do you have to wait?"

Jillian shook her head. "For some reason I don't understand, Dwayne managed to get me in next week."

"Wow! That's fast."

"I know. If everything comes out all right—and Dwayne seems to think it will—I might be able to go back to work the week after next. I'll have to be supervised. . . ." She cast her glance downward then looked up with a smile. "But that's probably for the best. My judgment obviously stinks."

"Give yourself some time, Jillian." Emily stood up to go. "I need to get back to the clinic. Call me when you hear any more news."

They hugged again at the door. "See you at church Sunday," Jillian said as Emily walked across the yard to the driveway.

Emily waved back and got into her car. She used the time driving to the clinic to reflect and pray. So much had happened in such a short time that she felt as though her head were spinning.

When she pulled into the parking lot, she saw a couple of cars in front of the clinic, so she hurried inside. Noah stood talking to one of the men by the front desk. He saw her and smiled.

"I'm glad you're back, Emily." His tone was more professional than usual.

She moved around behind the counter and settled into her chair beside Kingston, who appeared to be in the exact same spot where she'd left him. He lifted his head to greet her with one of his throaty sounds but quickly lay back down. "Is there something I can do?"

Noah offered a clipped nod. "Emily, I'd like you to meet Jerry and Gary, brothers who just moved into their parents' house to run the family farm."

Emily extended her hand. "Nice to meet you." She wasn't sure what was expected of her, so she let Noah take the lead.

"Would you set up a farm account for them?"

"Oh, yes of course." She felt stupid, but she'd never done this before.

Noah pointed to a box. "There are some cards in there that they can fill out." He turned to one of the men. "I'll come out to your place on whatever schedule is convenient for you. If there's an emergency, just call my cell phone and I'll be there as quickly as I can. We bill monthly."

The men exchanged a glance then turned to Noah. "Fine," Gary said. "Jerry will be out of town the rest of this week, but he'll be back on Monday. Why don't you come out next week?"

"Sounds good. Just give me a call and let me know what day."

After the men left, Noah answered questions from the lady who'd been waiting. He even told her how much he charged to examine dogs. Once everyone was gone, Noah turned and grinned at Emily, looking proud of himself. "Did I do okay?"

She tilted her head and looked at him in confusion. "What do you mean by that?"

"I mentioned billing and fees. I figured that way, they wouldn't be surprised when they got one of your letters."

Emily laughed. "I think most people expect to pay for veterinary services."

Noah did an about-face. "I need to head on back and see about those chickens."

After he left, Emily began to work on getting the mailing list for the new billing letter, when suddenly Kingston scrambled to his feet and started growling. That was weird.

"Kingston, what's wrong?"

He ran over to the supply closet and barked a couple of times before glancing back at Emily as if he wanted something. A low growl vibrated from his throat before he started barking again.

Noah stuck his head out. "What's going on out there?"

"I don't know. He just started this random barking."

Kingston stared at the door, still growling, so Emily got up and opened the supply closet door. That was when she caught a whiff of an awful smell.

As calmly as she could, Emily turned to Noah. "Either we have a gas leak, or someone's trying to burn the place down."

ten

"Quick! We need to get the animals out!" Noah shouted. "Grab the leash and take Kingston first. You can hook him on that tree out back." The urgency in his voice startled Emily into quick action.

The two of them ran back and forth, carrying cages of animals, the smell of the gas growing stronger as the minutes passed. Chickens squawked, the kittens mewed, but Kingston stood guard over them until all of them were under the tree—including Emily and Noah.

"Got your personal belongings?" Noah asked.

Her eyebrows shot up. "My purse is inside."

"I'll go get it." Noah ran back in before she had a chance to tell him not to worry about it.

When he didn't come out after a couple of minutes, Emily panicked. She ran toward the building and opened the front door. The odor of gas was so pungent she had to close it. By now she could smell it outside. Where was Noah?

She took a couple of steps back and deeply inhaled. Then she opened the door again and hollered Noah's name. No answer.

What if something happened to him? What if he fell? Her purse had been behind the reception counter near the front door, so he should have been out by now.

Emily started to bolt back in, but the next thing she knew, Noah was running toward her, handbag slung over one arm and a tiny kitten in the other hand. She ran out of the way, and he bolted out the door right behind her.

"I heard a noise when I went in for your purse," he said as he handed it to her. "I couldn't leave this innocent little creature behind." He rubbed the top of her head with one finger. "She'd somehow gotten out of the box and crawled beneath one of the cabinets. I had a hard time getting her out."

That was one fortunate kitten. "You scared me half to death, Noah."

"Sorry." He walked around the animals and checked to make sure they were okay. Kingston sat there watching every move Noah made.

Emily opened her handbag and pulled out her cell phone to call 911. The dispatcher told her not to go back inside for any reason—not even something valuable—because the building could blow up. She knew that, but hearing it come from an authority figure made her dizzy.

When Emily reached out and touched Noah's arm for comfort, he immediately pulled her into his arms for an embrace. It felt natural to be there. Emily allowed herself to bask in his warmth for a moment, but then she came to her senses and pulled away.

Noah gave her a puzzled look. "Emily. . ."

As the sound of sirens drew near, Emily turned to Noah. "What do you think happened?"

"Who knows? I guess we'll find out soon enough."

It took more than an hour before the fire department had an answer for them. They had to be cautious as they approached the building. Eventually one of the firefighters came over to where Noah and Emily waited with the animals.

"The line to the water heater in the closet had burst. We had to turn off the gas." He rubbed his neck. "That was some gas leak. Y'all were fortunate the place didn't blow up." He looked around at the animals. "You got all of them out? Man, you took a huge chance with your lives."

"We had to," Emily replied. "We couldn't just leave them in there."

"That was mighty risky. There was so much gas in there,

another five minutes and this place would most likely have blown to bits."

⁊⁊

Noah inwardly shuddered as he considered what could have happened. Emily hadn't hesitated to run back into the building—not only for the animals but to look for him. That had to mean something. But then he remembered her reaction when he'd pulled her close. He'd acted on instinct—something he'd have to control in the future.

After the firefighter gave them the go-ahead to carry all the animals back inside, Noah told Emily to sit down and let him do it. "You've done enough already."

She cast a you've-got-to-be-kidding look in his direction. "No way. I'm not letting you do all this by yourself."

An image of Tiffany sitting and watching him move all her furniture into her new apartment while she supervised flitted through his mind.

"I appreciate all this, Emily. You've been amazing."

"Anyone would do this," she shot back. "Now let's get all those chickens back inside." She turned to the Great Dane. "I'll be right back for you, buddy."

It took them longer to get the animals back inside than it had to carry them out. Noah realized they must have been operating on adrenaline.

On the firefighter's advice, he called a plumber to replace the water heater. They promised to be there that afternoon.

Once the animals were all back in their rightful places, Emily looked up at Noah. "Never a dull moment around here, is there?"

He let out a chuckle. "You could say that."

She grinned. "I just did."

Noah felt an emotional tug as Emily positioned herself back behind the reception counter. He went about his business, with her and her bravery on his mind. Despite the danger, he suspected she would do it all over again.

After examining the first chicken, he put her back then picked up the next one. A glimmer of something white caught his eye. He reached his hand into the cage and pulled out an egg.

Holding the chicken in front of his face, he smiled. "So it takes a little excitement to get you to do your job, huh?"

The chicken made a few jerky movements with her head, but she refused to look him in the eye. He put her back in her cage and got the next one. He was happy to learn there was absolutely nothing wrong with any of the chickens.

He went out and told Emily to get Mack on the phone.

"Are the chickens okay?" she asked.

"They're fine. I suspect they're just molting. It's natural, and they generally take a break from laying because they have to put all their energy into feather growth."

Emily laughed as she picked up the phone. "We wouldn't want a naked chicken, would we?"

"No," Noah agreed. "That would be scandalous."

"Hopefully Mack can pick up the chickens before I leave today."

"Yeah, I don't want to have to worry about them after the scare we had."

"Me either."

The rest of the day was fairly routine, which was just fine with Noah. He didn't need any more excitement for a while. The plumber installed a new water heater and attached a gizmo that would detect a gas leak and sound an alarm.

࿇

On Sunday morning, Aunt Sherry beamed at Emily from her normal spot by the stove. "We've been blessed with the task of picking up Jillian for church."

Emily grinned back. She loved how her aunt saw everything as a blessing. "It'll be fun."

"I have to admit, when Dwayne first called and identified himself, I was worried something else had happened."

"That's understandable, considering how much crazy news we've had lately."

Aunt Sherry laughed as she turned back to the stove to tend to the eggs. "I'm just glad Kingston was at the clinic to sniff out the gas before it was too late."

At the sound of his name, Kingston rounded the corner and came to a sliding halt at the entrance of the kitchen. He tilted his head, as if to ask if someone had called for him. Both women laughed.

"Good boy," Aunt Sherry said as she reached into a container and pulled out a jerky treat. He looked at Emily, who nodded, then he didn't waste another minute before getting his treat. "I've heard that a dog's sense of smell is hundreds of times greater than a human's."

"I'm sure we would have smelled it eventually," Emily said. "It was pretty strong, once we opened the closet door. I'm just glad Kingston caught it soon enough for us to get all the animals out."

"That's good. You just never know about things like that. I'm thankful it turned out okay."

They ate breakfast and left for church as soon as Mel was ready. "Do you know where this girl lives?" he asked.

Emily gave him directions. Jillian was waiting by the door, so she ran out to the car as soon as they got there.

"You look nice, Jillian," Aunt Sherry said. "I love your dress."

A look of panic shot across Jillian's face as she glanced around at everyone else. "Did I overdress?"

"No," Aunt Sherry said. "Most of the time I dress up, but I figured I'd wear slacks today. You'll see people in everything from frilly frocks to jeans."

Frilly frocks. Now that's funny.

When Jillian looked at her with a half smile, it took everything Emily had not to crack up. Uncle Mel caught her gaze in the rearview mirror, and she could see the smile playing in his eyes, too.

Noah stood at the church entrance waiting, so when they walked up, he shook Uncle Mel's hand and gave the rest of them a hug. Since Emily was last, he kept his hand on her shoulder as they went inside. Emily felt like part of a couple—which she enjoyed much more than she should have, considering Noah was her boss.

It felt natural to be with him, yet she tingled at his touch. She never wanted him to remove his hand, but once Uncle Mel found a pew with enough room for all of them, he let go and gestured for her to move ahead of him.

Since Jillian hadn't been to church much, Emily helped familiarize her with the order of service. She showed her the hymnals they'd use and pointed to the large overhead screen at the front of the church. "That's for the words of the more contemporary songs," she explained. "I don't know all of them, so I usually listen to the first verse. Then I join in after I know the tune."

Jillian nodded. "That makes sense."

Emily could see Jillian's hands shaking, so she reached over and gave her a squeeze. Hopefully Jillian would agree to return—that is, if she didn't get into more trouble.

When Emily turned back, she saw that someone had joined them on the other side of Noah. "Oh hi, Dwayne."

He grinned and lifted his hand in a wave. Then when he leaned forward and made eye contact with Jillian, she saw Dwayne's compassion, and that instantly made her heart melt.

After the service, Noah asked if she and Jillian would like to join him and Dwayne for a walk around Pullman Square.

She turned to Aunt Sherry, who waved her hand. "Y'all go and have a good time. If you get hungry, there's always plenty of food at our place."

Noah chuckled. "I just finished the leftovers you brought from last week."

"You can come by and pick up some more for next week,"

Mel said with a snort. "Sherry cooks up a storm on Sundays. She doesn't know when to stop."

"Why, Mel, this is the first time I've ever heard you complain!"

He winked at his wife. "Oh, I'm not complaining. I'm just sayin'...."

Emily gave her aunt and uncle a hug before returning to her friends. Noah used his eyes and a tilt of his head to turn her attention to Dwayne and Jillian, who were chatting. Emily suspected Dwayne was giving his testimony, and she relaxed. Jillian was in good hands with these wonderful people.

"Do you think there's something going on between them?" Emily whispered.

Noah slowly smiled and shrugged. "Not overtly, but maybe on a subconscious level. Wouldn't that be an interesting twist?" A more pensive look covered his face. "He needs to be careful. We've gotten close, and he admitted that he's attracted to vulnerable women. Maybe it's his protective instincts."

"Yes," Emily agreed, "he does need to be very careful." Emily grinned back. "You can't find a finer man than Dwayne. He's a deputy for all the right reasons. He wants to help this community."

They walked around Pullman Square then left to have lunch at a diner not far away. The entire time, Jillian and Dwayne chatted nonstop. Emily overheard Dwayne witnessing to Jillian.

"Wanna go for a little walk?" Noah asked.

"Sure."

After letting Dwayne and Jillian know that they were heading off on their own and assuring Dwayne they wouldn't be long, Noah took Emily's hand and led her down a different path. She pointed out some flowers and trees that she'd love to paint.

"You ought to come up here sometime and set up your easel," Noah said.

"I'd like to do that." When she turned to face Noah, she

saw his features softening. "What are you thinking about?"

"Really wanna know?" His bottom lip twitched.

"Yeah."

He took her hands in his, forcing her to turn to face him. "I really like you, Emily."

"I like you, too, Noah."

"I mean I *really* like you. I think we're good together."

Emily swallowed hard. She didn't know what to do, so she blinked a couple of times then pointed in the direction they'd come from. "I think we need to head on back."

"I guess I know how you feel now."

"Noah, I have strong feelings for you, too, but I'm still going back and forth on what to do with my life. It wouldn't be fair to you if we allowed our feelings to develop into more than what they are."

He snickered. "I guess you're right. Let's get on back. They're probably wondering where we are anyway."

By the time they got back to Dwayne's car, Emily's heart had slowed to a more normal pace. Dwayne gave them an odd look then chuckled and shook his head.

"Any idea when you'll be able to come back to work?" Noah asked Jillian.

"Are you sure you want me back?"

Noah didn't hesitate to nod. "Absolutely, yes. You made a mistake that will affect you for a long time, but I don't think you intended to hurt me. Hopefully you learned to stay away from bad dudes."

"You got that right."

Noah couldn't help but notice Dwayne's protective gaze toward Jillian. "So back to my question. Any idea when?"

She glanced at Dwayne before shaking her head. "Not sure yet. If everything goes like I hope, I'll be able to finish out the semester at school and go back to work soon."

Emily figured it was time for her to say something. "I'll be able to fill in until you can return."

"I appreciate that," Jillian said. "How much longer do you think you'll be around?"

All eyes were now on Emily, forcing her to answer a question that had been playing in her mind since she arrived. "That's a tough one to call," she said slowly. "I still don't know what the Lord wants me to do."

Noah's eyes narrowed, and an odd expression crossed his face. Was it a look of concern, or was it disapproval? She suddenly felt self-conscious.

Dwayne held up his hands. "We'll pray about it then," he said. "I've seen Him answer my prayers in ways that I never would have imagined." He looked down at Jillian who nodded.

There was no doubt in Emily's mind that Dwayne wanted to do everything in his power to help Jillian. However, it was hard to tell what was going on with Jillian, other than the fact that she'd royally messed up her life and needed to spend every waking moment getting it back in order. At least she'd agreed to go to church.

As they settled into Dwayne's car and buckled their seat belts, Emily thought about how everyone's lives seemed to be in a state of turmoil. She'd once thought she was the only person who didn't have her act together, but as she looked around the car, she realized she'd been mistaken.

Jillian's chaos was obvious. She was still in school but not even certain about whether or not she could continue with the semester. Her former boyfriend was a drug dealer, and he didn't mind using her to get what he wanted. And now the attraction between her and Dwayne cast a whole new light on her life.

Dwayne had been a sheriff's deputy for four years, and today Emily had learned that he aspired to move up to a detective position with the child services department. He wanted to save kids from suffering as he had in foster care.

Even Noah had issues that she suspected had something to

do with his former fiancée. Maybe one of these days she'd get him to open up.

"Do y'all mind if I take Jillian home first?" Dwayne asked, jolting her from her thoughts. "I managed to get permission for her to go to church and out to lunch afterward. I don't want to push things." He glanced at his watch. "We're close to her curfew."

"No, of course we don't mind," Noah replied. He looked at Emily.

Emily shook her head. "I don't mind."

Jillian turned around toward Emily and Noah. "I had the best time today. After hanging out with Brad, I almost forgot what it was like to be a normal person."

"How did you and Brad meet?" Emily asked. "I can't imagine someone like you getting involved with someone like him."

"He came by one day with a friend who needed to discuss something with my mom. Mom and that other guy left for a while, so Brad and I started talking. I thought he was pretty nice, and to be honest, I was a little attracted to his bad-boy image." Jillian paused for a moment.

Emily nodded. She'd known other girls who liked guys who lived on the edge.

"Anyway, one thing led to another, and the next thing you know, he and I were hanging out every weekend."

"Did you have any idea he sold drugs?" Emily asked.

"No, but I did know he used them." She licked her lips and grimaced. "That's the main reason I broke up with him. It created a big mess."

Noah cleared his throat and gave her a firm look. "I hope you stay broken up with him this time."

Jillian offered a half smile. "Trust me, I will. I don't need someone like Brad in my life. If he ever gets out of jail, I'll be more prepared for something like this. He caught me off guard."

Dwayne turned to her and nodded. "There are plenty of nice guys to pick from."

After they made the last turn onto Jillian's road, she gasped as she reached out and grabbed Dwayne's arm. "Don't stop."

"Huh?"

She pointed to the car parked in front of her house. "That's Brad's car."

eleven

Emily's throat constricted as she glanced at Noah then Dwayne. He tightened his jaw. "We can't run from him."

Noah leaned forward. "But I thought he was still in jail."

"Someone probably posted bond." Dwayne's shoulders sagged as he slowed down. "We didn't think anyone would."

Jillian shook her head. "He has some friends with money. I'm just surprised any of them came through for him."

"Are you afraid?" Dwayne asked as he glanced over toward Jillian.

She hesitated then nodded. "A little."

Dwayne pulled up in front of her house. "I'll go up with you and make sure everything's okay."

"Want me to come with you?" Noah asked.

"Nah, I don't think that would be such a good idea." Dwayne patted his pocket. "I have my cell phone right here. If I don't come out in five minutes, call me."

As soon as she and Noah were alone, Emily let out the breath she'd been holding. "This is too weird."

"Yes, I know. I feel sorry for Jillian." Noah leaned over and looked at her house. "She's a nice girl who stumbled over the wrong guy. I've seen it happen before."

"Yeah, me, too," Emily whispered. She looked down at her watch. "How long has it been now?"

Noah smiled and patted her arm. "About two minutes."

Emily turned and looked directly into Noah's eyes. Something strange but wonderful flashed between them, and her stomach felt like it was on a free fall. His tenderness and concern stirred the chemistry between them. She cleared her throat.

"Waiting is never fun, is it?" Noah asked.

Emily swallowed hard as she thought how she'd waited for her mother who never returned. Based on her experience, waiting was always miserable.

"Emily?" He gently touched her face.

She turned to face him. "No, waiting isn't fun. Not when we're worried about someone we like." She straightened her shoulders then paused before adding, "Want to call Dwayne, or do you want me to?"

Noah took her hand in his and squeezed it. "Let's say a prayer, then I'll make the call."

As they bowed their heads in prayer, Emily felt a warm tenderness as it surged through her. Noah consistently ignited something in her that she'd never before experienced. There was no doubt in her mind that he genuinely cared for her. But he cared about Jillian, too, so maybe he saw her as nothing more than another friend in need.

Noah finished his prayer for guidance and safety. As they said "Amen," Emily slowly lifted her head and opened her eyes, only to catch him staring at her.

"You okay?" he asked, a new softness in his voice. "I don't want you to be afraid."

As long as Noah was by her side, she didn't feel an ounce of fear. She smiled back. "I'm fine."

Noah punched in Dwayne's number and held the phone to his ear. After several rings and no answer, he frowned. "This isn't good."

"You don't think. . . ?" Emily's voice trailed off as she tried to block out the possibility of something bad happening.

"I don't know," he replied. "Let me try once more before I do anything."

He called Dwayne's number again. After a few seconds his face lit up and he winked before talking. "Hey, man, I was worried about you when you didn't answer."

Emily watched Noah's face as he listened to Dwayne. As

his smile faded to concern, her heart sank. Noah clicked his phone shut and pursed his lips.

"What happened?"

Noah lowered his head then turned and looked at her. "Dwayne says he's not leaving until Brad leaves."

"Why doesn't he just tell Brad to get out?"

"Apparently Jillian's mother is in there complicating matters." His forehead crinkled. "He acted like he couldn't talk."

"Should we do something?" Emily asked. "I mean, we can't just sit here."

Noah chewed on his bottom lip for a moment before nodding. "I'm not sure yet."

"Want me to. . ." The sight of Jillian's front door opening caught her attention.

Noah turned, and they both saw a strange man coming out of the house, with Dwayne close behind. As they got closer, Emily noticed the flash of handcuffs on the man's wrists.

"Uh-oh." Emily turned to Noah. "Looks like we have a situation."

"You stay here while I go find out what's going on." Noah looked at her with his head tilted forward. "I don't want to take a chance on anything happening to you."

Her heart pounded as she pulled her lips between her teeth and nodded. "I'll be right here."

Emily forced herself to remain calm as she watched Noah get out of the car and walk toward Dwayne, who still hadn't let go of the man she assumed was Brad. The situation seemed dangerous, and Noah had no idea what he was getting into. Jillian hadn't shown her face, which seemed odd to Emily.

She watched as Noah and Dwayne discussed something that caused Brad to scowl. All her attention focused on the one hand Dwayne had on Brad, whose arms were hidden behind his back.

Finally, after what seemed like forever, Noah issued a

clipped nod then headed back to the car. "Looks like Brad's going back to jail. Dwayne said he'll be able to take us home as soon as his backup arrives."

Emily felt a surge of relief as the squad car arrived, lights flashing but silent. A couple of police officers hopped out, relieving Dwayne so he could go back to his car.

As soon as he got in and closed the car door, Dwayne shook his head. "That guy is bad news. Everything would have been okay if he'd stayed away, but he's a time bomb."

"What happened?" Emily asked. "Can you talk about it?"

"He threatened Jillian and her mother in front of me. That's all I can say right now. We have some people on their way here to see about Jillian and her mother."

Emily turned to Noah and shook her head before refocusing her attention on Dwayne. "Is Jillian okay?"

"A little shaken," Dwayne replied, "but otherwise okay. I told her I'd call later and maybe stop by if she didn't mind." He cleared his throat before adding, "Just to make sure she's not scared."

"I'm just glad no one was hurt," Noah said.

Dwayne snickered. "You and me both."

Noah changed the subject and chatted about the message during church. Emily could tell he did that on purpose to relieve Dwayne of the stress from the confrontation.

ᔰ

After they dropped Emily off at Mel and Sherry's place, Noah turned to Dwayne. "So what really happened in there?"

Dwayne flinched. "Do you really wanna know?"

"Yes, of course."

"He had a knife at Jillian's mother's throat."

Noah shuddered. "I figured it was worse than you let on. Thanks for not giving the details in front of Emily. She's worried about Jillian enough as it is."

Dwayne shook his head. "I don't know what Jillian ever saw in that guy. She's cute and smart. He's dark and dangerous."

"I understand he's an actor, too. Jillian said she had no idea how bad of a guy he was until after she was involved."

"Yeah," Dwayne agreed. "Guys like that are con artists. That's how they get what they want, but it eventually catches up with them."

"Do you think Jillian will be safe coming back to work at the clinic?" Noah asked.

"She will be as long as Brad stays in jail."

"I don't want to do anything that'll endanger her life." Noah folded his arms as he thought for a moment. "I'll ask Emily if she can stay on full-time until we know what's going on with Brad."

As they approached the stop sign, Dwayne turned to Noah and grinned. "I have a feeling she won't mind staying as long as you want her."

Noah felt a rush of joy, but he quickly squelched it. "She's a nice woman, but I don't want her to think I'm taking advantage of her."

"Any idea what she plans to do?" Dwayne asked. "Mel said she's having a hard time finding herself."

"She doesn't say much about it. All I know is what she told me—that she's trying to figure out what to do with her life."

"It's tough." Dwayne paused for a few seconds. "I've known all my life I wanted to be a cop." He cast a quick glance Noah's way. "How about you?"

"I've always wanted to take care of animals. I went through a short period when I thought I might want to be a rancher, but it's tough to make a living at that on a small scale these days."

"Tell me about it," Dwayne groused. "My folks have been trying to sell their ranch for a fraction of what it was worth ten years ago. So far, the only possibility is the man who owns the land next to them. Dad doesn't want to sell to him because the guy hasn't always been honest, but he might not have a choice."

"All we can do is pray about it and leave it in the Lord's hands."

"Amen to that, brother."

After Noah got home, he thought about a plan to discuss with Emily. Having her full-time worked out well for him, but she couldn't go on indefinitely. He needed to find out when Jillian might be able to return and have a backup plan in case she couldn't.

He was the first to arrive at the clinic early the next morning. Emily walked in a half hour later, Kingston at her heels.

"Kingston." Noah patted the dog on the head and got a slurp on the arm in return. Then he turned to Emily. "Hey there."

"Good morning," she said. "How's Jillian?"

"I don't know yet. I figured I'd call later on if we don't hear something soon."

"Did Dwayne have any idea when she'd be safe from Brad?"

Noah leaned against the counter. "They're trying to push up his court date. If he's convicted, he'll go to prison for a while, since this isn't his first offense. Then Jillian can breathe easy—at least until he gets out."

"He won't stay out long, I'm sure," Emily said. "Unless he has a major life conversion, I can't see someone like that changing."

"As hard as it is, we need to pray for him."

"Any appointments this morning?" Emily asked.

"Not until ten. But there's something I'd like to discuss with you."

Emily's heart pounded as she met Noah's expectant gaze. She licked her lips and forced a smile. "Sure. Discuss away."

"I know you've been trying to figure out what you want to do, so I hate to ask you this favor. Since Jillian obviously can't come back until she's safe from Brad, would you consider staying on full-time—at least for a little while longer?"

She slowly nodded. "I can do that. After all, they're trying to schedule the court date soon, so it shouldn't be too long."

Noah frowned but quickly recovered. "Yeah, it shouldn't be too long." He straightened up and stepped away from the counter before he stopped and steadied his gaze on her. "Any idea yet what you might do after you leave here?"

"I'd like to do something with my degree, but most of the jobs I've applied for want a master's, and I only have my bachelor's."

"Why don't you go back to school?"

Emily made a face. "To be honest, I'm sick of school. I worked hard to finish so I could get a good job, but with the economy like it is, that isn't enough anymore."

"Did you know what you wanted to do when you first started college?" he asked. "When you told me you majored in art history, I wasn't sure what kind of job you could get with that."

She closed her eyes then opened them as she offered a dreamy grin. "I thought it would be fun to work as a curator at an art museum in New York or Chicago."

"So you want to move to the big city, huh?"

Once upon a time that was exactly what she wanted, but she wasn't so sure anymore. "I really don't know what I want." She held up her hands and shrugged. "And without my master's, well. . ." Her voice trailed off.

"We have some decent colleges around here," Noah said. "If you decide to go for your master's, I'm sure Mel and Sherry would love for you to stay with them." He paused before adding, "And as long as you're in town, I'll always have a job for you."

That actually sounded good, but if she went back to school, it would have to be one with a better-known art program. Then there was the fact that Emily loved working with Noah, in spite of the fact that she wasn't using her education.

"I'll think about it. Thank you."

Noah flashed a full smile her way. "I mean it. Just let me know. Hopefully Jillian will be back soon, so you can go back to being part-time and not have to spend your whole day here."

Emily felt a flash of annoyance with herself for thinking it wouldn't be so bad to spend entire days at the clinic. After all, she didn't need her degree for that.

"Let me know if you change your mind," he said softly. "I'm never sure what you're thinking—or if you're just doing things because you're trying to be nice."

"What's wrong with trying to be nice?" The instant the words came out, she realized she'd snapped. "Sorry."

He held her gaze for several seconds before blinking. "I'm the one who should apologize."

As soon as Noah left her and Kingston alone, Emily got right to work on pulling up the files of people who owed Noah's Ark money. Starting with the highest dollar amount first, she generated a billing plan that would enable people to at least knock out some of what they owed.

After she had a large stack of envelopes ready to take to the post office, she boxed them up and stuck them in a corner so Noah could take a look at them. The next few hours flew by.

As soon as the last morning appointment left, Emily ducked into the room where she knew Noah would be cleaning. "Got a minute?"

He glanced up and nodded. "Sure. Be right there."

Emily paused and watched his strong shoulders as he wiped down the surfaces with care. Noah was good at what he did, and his clients were fortunate to have him. She hated that some of them might be taking advantage of his generosity.

After he looked at her and grinned, she smiled back and headed back to her desk. A few minutes later he joined her. "What's up?"

She pulled the envelopes toward her. "I'd like to send out the bills this afternoon, but I wanted you to glance at them first."

Noah's jaw pulsed as he stared at the stack. Even after agreeing to do it, she knew it grated on him to pursue collection on the accounts.

"This is just a subtle prompt to jog their memory about the money they owe you," she reminded him, "and I offered a payment plan so it shouldn't be too hard for any of them, and. . ." She caught herself rambling. "Here," she said, as she lifted the top envelope and handed it to him. "See for yourself."

He opened it and pulled out the paper. As his gaze raked over the paper, Emily held her breath, hoping he'd give her the go-ahead to mail it.

"You didn't change anything, right?" he asked.

She nodded. "The smaller amounts are on a six-month plan. The higher amounts are broken down into one-year and two-year payback plans. And the first due date gives folks a few weeks to work it into their monthly budget."

After a short pause, he finally agreed. "I hate strong-arming people, but you're right—they do owe me for services. I should have done this sooner."

"It's not like you're threatening them or anything," she added.

Finally he chuckled. "Yeah, let's send them out and see what happens. If anyone can't pay, I'm sure we'll either hear from them or they'll just stop calling."

"I don't think that'll happen," Emily said. "If they have animals, they obviously need a vet."

"You're right." Noah stood and continued staring at her, making her feel very uncomfortable.

She reached up and tucked her hair behind her ear. "I'll mail these during lunch."

"I appreciate it, Emily." He pulled his lips between his teeth then opened his mouth to say something else when the phone rang.

With a smile, she lifted the receiver. "Good morning. Noah's Ark. May I help you?"

Noah waved good-bye then headed for the door. He'd switched his schedule for the day to meet the needs of his clients, which was why he needed someone at the clinic all the time. Emily felt an internal tug, watching him leave.

అ

Given everything he had to work with, Noah was doing the best he could to keep his feelings for Emily in check. For the past several years he'd watched friends he'd grown up with fall in love, one by one, until he was the last bachelor left. He didn't understand what they meant when they said they couldn't imagine life without the women they chose to spend the rest of their lives with—until now. Even with Tiffany he hadn't felt that all-consuming need.

Emily was special. She cared about everyone she was around—him, Jillian, the animals, her aunt and uncle. It was almost like she thought she was solely responsible for their happiness.

On his way out to the first farm visit, he decided to stop by and see Dwayne at the sheriff's department. He needed to find out if Brad's court date had been set yet.

As Noah pulled into the parking lot, he noticed the tiny red Subaru. He found a spot then walked past the car he thought might be Jillian's and looked in. Yep, those were her textbooks. It was hers. What was she doing at the sheriff's department?

twelve

Noah spotted Dwayne the second he walked into the lobby of the station. Jillian stood in front of Dwayne with her back to the door.

"What are you doing here?" Noah asked. "I thought you weren't allowed to go anywhere without permission."

Jillian tilted her head and gave him a you're-kidding look. "I obviously have permission to be here."

Noah snickered. "Good point. Any word yet?"

Jillian turned around and smiled. "They're still working on the court date."

"It won't be long though." Dwayne glanced at Jillian then quickly looked up at Noah.

"I'll sure be glad when everything's back to normal," Noah said. "Emily agreed to work full-time until Brad's behind bars for good and Jillian can return."

Jillian offered a sympathetic grin. "I'm really sorry, Noah. It's all my fault."

Dwayne narrowed his eyes. "Guys like Brad are con artists. They prey on nice people—especially nice, vulnerable girls. You had no way of knowing that."

Noah found it charming that Dwayne was defensive toward Jillian. Under different circumstances, he could see the two of them in a more romantic relationship. It could still happen, but Jillian needed to work through some serious issues first.

"Tell Emily I'll call her later," Jillian said before she turned back to Dwayne. "I have to run to class now. They're letting me sit in on a later class to catch up."

After Jillian left, Noah turned back to Dwayne. "She's a sweet girl."

"Yeah." Dwayne stared at the door, as though her image were still there.

"Too bad you met her at such a difficult time."

He slowly turned to Noah and nodded. "Yeah, I thought that, too. But I have time. I'm still in my twenties." Dwayne paused for a moment. "So, what brings you here?"

"I just wanted to see when I could get Jillian back. As long as there's a chance Brad will get out, I can't let her have the key to the clinic."

"Yeah, the temptation for Brad to come after her is too great as long as he thinks she can open the door to the narcotics," Dwayne agreed.

Noah took a step toward the door then stopped. "After this thing is all behind us and Brad's safely locked away in the penitentiary, the four of us need to celebrate."

"So I was right," Dwayne said, a smug look on his face as he crossed his arms.

"Right about what?"

"You and Emily." He grinned. "You like her a lot, don't you?"

"Emily and I are friends, if that's what you're saying." Noah couldn't look Dwayne in the eye, but he didn't want to create a problem for Emily. Besides, what was the point in starting a rumor about even a hint of a relationship between him and Emily when she was likely to leave after she figured out where she wanted to go?

"Right." Dwayne snickered.

Noah lifted his hands. "Okay, so I think she's cute."

Dwayne lifted an eyebrow and pursed his lips. "And?"

"Well. . ." Noah pondered what else to say. "She's smart and fun."

"That's what I thought. You can't deny it," Dwayne said, a wide grin spread across his face. "You're smitten."

"Smitten." Noah shook his head. "Now that's a word I haven't heard in a while." He snickered. "Well, okay, so what if I am?"

"At least you're finally admitting it."

"Yeah." Noah shoved his hands in his pockets and looked around before settling his look on Dwayne. "It must've been rough seeing Jillian behind bars. I can't picture it."

Dwayne shook his head. "You don't know the half of it. I stood on one side of the bars with her on the other, and I didn't know what to say. She looked so fragile and helpless, and there wasn't a thing I could do about it." He chewed his bottom lip as the lines in his forehead deepened. "I've seen a lot of people in jail, but this one really got me."

Noah felt terrible for Jillian. She didn't deserve many of the things she'd experienced in life. He had no doubt that the Lord had crossed their paths for a reason, and he didn't want to miss an opportunity to be a gentle, loving witness. Obviously Dwayne felt the same way.

"At least she knows she has us on her side."

Dwayne tightened his lips across his teeth, showing his continued frustration. "We talked a few times, and she was very open about her past. Her problems started early. She's been through a lot, and her mother was never a good one to give her direction."

"Not everyone has good parents. Thankfully Jesus has given us grace and the opportunity to change things through faith."

"You're so right." Dwayne hooked his thumbs through the belt loops of his uniform. "Jillian seemed to like church."

Noah smiled and nodded. "I think so."

"Like you said, the four of us will have to get together." Dwayne looked at Noah with expectation.

"Sounds good." Noah had run out of things to say, and he suddenly felt awkward. "Emily and Jillian get along great, so we might even hang out for a whole day."

"After this thing with Brad is settled," Dwayne reminded him.

"That goes without saying." Noah took a step toward the door. "I have a few farm calls to make, then I want to get back to the clinic."

"At least you get to see Emily every day."

"True," Noah agreed, "but I'm not sure she's all that happy about it."

"She might not realize it, but I think she's very happy to see you. I can see it on her face."

On that note, Noah chuckled and waved good-bye to his buddy. He was glad to have a Christian friend he could talk to.

ја

After she dropped off the bills at the post office, Emily stopped at a deli and grabbed a sandwich to take back to work with her. She couldn't take Kingston inside, and she wasn't about to leave him in the car.

Between the constantly ringing phone and the paperwork that needed filing, Emily stayed busy, and the afternoon flew. When Noah returned, she glanced up at the clock. It was almost closing time already.

She handed him his messages then turned back to her computer. He didn't move away from the counter, so she glanced up at him, only to catch him staring back at her. Suddenly he seemed flustered.

"Did you need something?" she asked.

"Um. . .oh, no, I just. . ." He chewed his bottom lip as he flipped through the messages. "If you're done for the day, why don't you go on home? I don't have any more appointments today."

"Are you sure?"

He nodded. "Positive. In fact, I think I might leave in a few minutes. I'm pretty booked tomorrow."

"Okay," she said as she slowly reached for her handbag beneath the counter. "I got the bills in the mail today."

Noah smiled through a groan. "Maybe you should plan to stay late for a few days—that is, if you don't have to be somewhere."

"I don't think it'll be too bad," she said.

"I should have been firm about it from the beginning. I

guess I was so busy with my clients' needs that I neglected my business."

"It'll be fine," Emily assured him. "If they balk, I'll do what I can to work it out." She glanced down then looked back up at him, feeling a little bit embarrassed. "Of course, that's only if you trust me enough to let me handle it. I didn't mean to be presumptuous."

"I do trust you, Emily." His look said more, but she couldn't hold his gaze too long without feeling an uncomfortable flutter inside.

"C'mon, Kingston," she said as she leaned over toward the dog. "Ready to go home?"

His ears perked up as he scrambled to his feet. Kingston's legs were long, and they seemed to tangle every time he lay down. The dog was so comical she had to smile.

"How's he been?" Noah asked. "Giving you any trouble?"

"No, not at all." Emily tucked her hair behind her ear with one hand and snapped the leash on Kinston's collar with the other. "In fact, I'll be sad when Mr. Zimmerman comes back and takes him away."

"I feel like you're safe as long as he's with you," Noah said.

"Yeah, me, too."

She felt Noah's gaze as she and Kingston walked toward the door. After one last good-bye wave, she guided the dog toward her car and got in. All the way to the farm, she alternated between praying and talking to Kingston, who listened with rapt attention.

The next morning, Emily and Kingston arrived at the clinic a half hour early. She wanted to get all her daily work done before the bills she'd sent arrived at Noah's clients' houses.

By midafternoon the calls had begun to trickle in, but none of them were bad. So far, all they wanted to know was if they could still continue using Noah's services before they'd paid in full. Emily assured them that they could, and she reminded them to read the entire message at the top of their bill. "We just wanted to make sure we were in agreement on your outstanding balance," she said.

Occasionally she caught Noah standing nearby, listening as she spoke to clients. After she hung up, he always gave her a thumbs-up and a heartwarming grin.

The next several weeks were busy for both Noah and Emily. The floodwaters had continued to recede, and he spent quite a bit of his time helping the farmers clean up the mess then moving their animals back. Soon Emily was up to her elbows in accounts receivable payments. Her hunch had proven to be correct—people didn't mind paying their bills; they just weren't sure what they owed, and they needed a nudge.

 a

As Noah's account grew, he saw what a valuable asset Emily was to his business. Back home, his father had always talked about how important the right front office help could be. Now he understood that. He'd never expected Jillian to do more than schedule appointments and greet clients when they came in for their appointments—and she was very good at that. However, Emily gave his office a more professional atmosphere, without making it seem stuffy. She was the perfect balance for his office.

"Noah."

He glanced up at the sound of his name. "Everything okay?"

Emily tilted her head and slowly moved it side to side. "Mrs. Anderson's cat fell out of a tree, and she thinks something's wrong with her."

"Bring her on back."

"I would, but we can't catch her."

Noah frowned. "Didn't she bring her in a cat carrier?"

"No, she had her in a box. As soon as she put the box on the floor, Muffin hopped out and ran."

"Let me see if I can catch her," Noah said as he put down the manual he'd been reading. "I've told Mrs. Anderson she really needs to invest in a carrier for Muffin. Poor kitty is scared half to death every time she comes here."

"Can you blame her?" Emily asked. "The only time Muffin ever goes out, she comes here and gets a shot. I'd be scared, too."

"Good point."

≈

Emily led the way back out to the reception room. As soon as Emily opened the door, she spotted Mrs. Anderson leaning over the reception counter, looking panic-stricken.

"Th–that beast is going to eat my little Muffin." She pointed. "Get her away from him."

When Emily rounded the corner and saw Kingston cuddling with the tiny cat, she smiled. "He won't hurt her, Mrs. Anderson. I think he's protecting her."

Noah came up from behind. "Great Danes are known as gentle giants," he explained. "They get along with other species quite well."

"B–but he's so big." Mrs. Anderson's eyes were still wide, and her face was drained of color. "He could hurt her."

"Kingston wouldn't want to hurt her." Noah bent over and picked up the cat then lifted her to his face so he could look her in the eye. "Did you make a new friend, Muffin?" He glanced up at Mrs. Anderson. "She seems fine, but I'll check her out anyway."

The cat's meow elicited a worried look from her owner. "I can't believe you let such a big dog run loose in here like that."

Emily smiled as she gently took Mrs. Anderson by the arm and led her around the counter, over to Kingston. "Look at that sweet face. He's a very friendly dog. Would you like to pet him?"

The older woman pondered that and frowned. "What if he doesn't like me?"

As if on cue, Kingston stood up and licked Mrs. Anderson's hand. She pulled back and giggled.

"See? He's very nice."

Mrs. Anderson carefully extended her hand for another lick, and she giggled again. Then she ran her hand over his head. "He does seem to be a friendly dog."

"He's very protective," Noah explained. "Dogs can sense fear in other animals, and since Muffin was afraid when she came in here, he wanted to look after her."

Mrs. Anderson's eyes glistened as she looked at Emily. "That's so sweet."

Emily felt ready to burst with pride, even though Kingston wasn't officially her dog. He was the sweetest animal she'd ever been around.

"Ready to go in for your checkup, Muffin?" Noah asked. He turned to her owner. "Would you like to come back with us?"

Mrs. Anderson looked over at Kingston and pointed. "Can he come with us?"

Emily turned to Noah, who nodded. "Sure, if that would make you feel better."

"I think it'll make Muffin feel better," Mrs. Anderson replied. As Noah, Muffin, Mrs. Anderson, and Kingston went back to the examining room, Emily heard the woman chattering. "Do you think I should get a dog for Muffin? How much do they eat? Where can I find a dog like this one?"

Emily smiled as she tried to imagine Mrs. Anderson having a dog the size of Kingston. Surely Noah would talk her out of it.

Fifteen minutes later the door opened and out walked Kingston, followed by Muffin. Emily could tell that Kingston was annoyed by the look on his face, but he didn't growl or snap. Instead, he headed straight for his bed behind the reception counter. Muffin plopped her little self down beside him. Kingston gave her a lick across the face, which got her motor purring. Within seconds Muffin's eyes closed and Kingston rested his chin on his front paw.

Mrs. Anderson still hadn't come out, and this concerned Emily. She waited a few minutes before she finally got up and went toward the examining room, where she heard Noah's voice. So she hunkered behind the wall and listened.

"I really don't think you need a dog the size of Kingston," Noah said. "In fact, getting a dog isn't the answer."

"But I've never seen her so happy," Mrs. Anderson argued.

"How much time do you spend with her?"

"As much as I can, but I still have things to do. Last time I came home from my bowling league, she'd shredded the curtains in the guest room."

"We can clip her nails," Noah said.

"I really want to get her a dog—"

Suddenly a sharp crashing sound jolted Emily from her perch behind the wall. She took off running toward the reception area to see what it was.

thirteen

"Uh-oh."

Emily stood at the door and surveyed the scene before her. Muffin was sprawled in the middle of a pile of dirt on the floor, with shards of a ceramic pot that had hung from the ceiling scattered over the floor, green leaves peeking out from beneath her. Kingston stood about five feet away, looking back and forth between Muffin and Emily, as though wondering what to do next.

"What happened?" Mrs. Anderson's voice was shrill with panic. "What did that beast do to my little Muffin?"

Noah came up right behind them. "Looks like Muffin decided to go for a ride on my plant." He squatted down beside the cat and stroked her fur. "She seems to be okay."

"My sweet little Muffin." Mrs. Anderson pointed at Kingston. "I'm sure it's his fault."

With a crooked grin, Noah stood up and planted his hands on his hips. "Still want to get her a dog?"

Muffin finally stood and shook the dirt off her fur, her ears cocked back in annoyance. Mrs. Anderson stepped back. "She's so dirty. Do something."

Emily spoke up. "I can give her a quick bath before you leave."

"She hates baths," Mrs. Anderson said.

"We have the right equipment." Noah lifted Muffin and handed her to Emily, who took her to the examining room with the deep sink. "It won't take her long," he added. "She's fast."

Fifteen minutes later, Mrs. Anderson and a much cleaner Muffin were out the door. The remains of the pot, plant, and dirt had been swept up and disposed of. Emily was glad

Noah had kept extra T-shirts in the supply closet because after Muffin's bath, she was a muddy mess.

Noah laughed. "I'm sort of glad that happened. I was concerned about her getting Muffin a dog, since she can barely care for the cat. I don't think we have to worry about that now."

Emily looked at Noah and felt her heart flutter. "There's definitely a silver lining to this."

His smile faded as he gazed at her. "I don't know what I would have done without you, Emily."

She opened her mouth to speak, but it was impossible with her heart pounding so hard she could hear it echoing in her head. Instead, she forced a smile and nodded.

"Would you like a soda?" Noah asked. "I filled the fridge with a variety."

"Sounds good," she managed to squeak. A soda was just the thing for her parched mouth.

After he left the reception area, Emily took a seat behind the counter and buried her face in her hands. She really needed to focus on what she was there for and stop harboring romantic thoughts about Noah. Neither of them needed a relationship—not Noah who was still trying to build his business and certainly not her, since she needed to figure out what she wanted before getting involved with a man.

He came back and handed her a can of Dr. Pepper. "How did you know this was what I'd want?"

Noah grinned. "Mel said he has to keep them in stock when you visit."

For the remainder of the day, Emily fielded calls that continued to straggle in about the bills. Then the mail came. A whole sack of it.

"Hang on to the bag, and I'll pick it up tomorrow," the mail carrier said.

"Thanks, Charlie."

After Charlie left, Emily started the task of opening each envelope and clipping each check to the bill. Noah wasn't in, so she entered the information in each client's file then prepared the deposit for Noah to drop off on his way home. Until now he'd made enough money to pay the bills and salaries from clients who paid at the time of service, but now there would be more, which would enable him to expand and hire additional assistants.

He finally arrived about fifteen minutes before she was due to leave. His eyes widened when he saw the deposit.

"Whoa." He picked up the stack and shook his head. "That's double the normal deposit. I see it, but I almost don't believe it."

"Believe it," she said. "All we had to do was ask."

"To be honest, I've never been good at collecting money people owed me." He plopped down in one of the chairs in the waiting room and stretched out his legs. "One of the guys I shared a house with in college once borrowed money to fix his car engine. I assumed he'd pay me back as soon as he got his next check, but the weeks went by, and he didn't hand over a dime."

"Why didn't you just ask him for it?"

"So much time had passed, and I couldn't find a way to do it."

"So how did you get your money back?" Emily asked.

"I didn't. He moved out at the end of the semester and left his furniture for the rest of us. I guess he figured that was his payment." Noah shrugged. "I knew he'd struggled with money all his life, and he went to school on student loans. It's especially hard for me to ask people for money that I know they don't have."

Emily liked that about Noah—his generous spirit. However, she also knew that some people would see it and take advantage of him if he didn't make an effort to collect.

Noah stood up and pointed to the deposit. "I'm grateful for all your hard work in getting this, Emily."

"I figure since I'm here anyway, I might as well earn my paycheck."

&

Noah was definitely indebted to Emily. Not only had she boosted his income, she'd managed to soothe nervous clients and patients when he felt frazzled. Emily wasn't just an employee; she was a valuable asset to his clinic. But he had to remind himself that he couldn't expect her to stick around much longer. She had her own dreams and aspirations, which certainly didn't include being a receptionist in a country vet clinic.

"Have you decided what to do about school?" he asked.

She averted her gaze. "Not really."

"Just remember, you can stay here as long as you want." He now knew that he wanted her forever, but he didn't want to confuse her even more.

When she turned back to face him, her eyes glistened with tears. Had he said something wrong?

"No pressure, okay?"

Emily swallowed hard and nodded. "I just feel like—I don't know—like I should know more about what I want out of life."

Noah bridged the gap between them and rested his elbows on the counter. The close proximity brought a sizzle to his nerves. "I know how difficult it can be. The only reason I knew what I wanted was that I loved hanging out in my dad's clinic ever since I can remember." He chuckled. "However, my favorite animals were the ones he hardly ever saw, which is why I'm here with the chickens, goats, and pigs."

Kingston stood up and audibly yawned. Emily laughed. "And Great Danes, right?"

Noah walked over to Kingston and rubbed behind his ears. "Absolutely. Great Danes and whatever else walks, flies, or slithers through that door."

Emily shuddered. "Thankfully I haven't seen much slithering since I've been here."

"Just wait," Noah said with a grin. "If you're here long enough, you'll see some slithering."

The instant those words were out of his mouth, he regretted saying them. He shouldn't have quantified her time with him—even with such a subtle reference to the future.

Emily offered a closed-mouth smile and quickly looked down. He wished he knew what she was thinking.

Kingston stood up, turned around, sat down next to him, then leaned his body against Noah's side. One side of the dog's jowl flopped open as he looked up at Noah.

"Whatcha thinkin', boy?" Noah asked as he scratched Kingston's head.

The dog sighed, which made Emily laugh. "He's in doggy heaven."

"I've never met a dog who didn't like having his ears or head scratched." Noah gently nudged Kingston away so he could go back to work. "But Kingston is probably the easiest one to please."

"He is absolutely the best dog I've ever been around," Emily admitted.

"Maybe you can talk Mr. Zimmerman into handing him over for good. He could be your companion until you leave. I'm sure Mel would love to have a dog like this." Noah looked her in the eye. "I've heard Mr. Zimmerman's thinking about selling his farm and moving to Florida."

"Why wouldn't he take Kingston with him?"

"He's too big to live in a condo."

"I can't imagine owning a farm all these years then moving to a condo," Emily said.

"It happens." Noah took a few more steps toward the examining area. "Maybe we'll know something when he gets back from Europe."

❧

After Noah left her alone in the reception area, Emily looked at Kingston, who stared at her with soulful eyes. She'd love to have Kingston for her own, but how would the dog feel about that? No doubt he was a loyal friend to Mr. Zimmerman.

Emily patted her leg. "C'mere, Kingston."

He dutifully closed the distance between them. Emily started to pat his head then decided to give him a hug instead. She leaned forward and pulled him toward her, allowing him to rest his chin on her shoulder. She didn't care if he slobbered down her back. All she knew was that it felt good to have the companionship she'd missed for so much of her life.

No matter how hard her dad had tried to be both a father and a mother to her, he was stretched so thin between his full-time and part-time jobs to keep a roof over their heads and food on the table that she rarely saw him. She'd spent many nights longing for her mother, knowing she'd been abandoned for a life of excitement. It still hurt and probably always would.

Emily would never forget when her dad came to her to break the news that her mother had left and wasn't coming back. At first she blamed her dad, thinking he'd done something to make her mother leave. But over time she realized that her father had nothing to do with it. If anything, his stability and faith in God had been what kept his wife there as long as she was.

"Your mother is a very confused woman," Aunt Sherry told her. "We pray for her every day, and you should, too."

At first Emily had a difficult time praying for someone who wanted nothing to do with her, but over time she realized how pitiful her mother's existence was. As an adult, Emily saw things differently. She'd learned more about her mother and understood that the woman had always teetered on the brink of disaster, and her father had pulled her out of a mess shortly after they met.

Emily's earliest memories of her mother were good. She and her dad went to church most Sundays, but her mother begged off due to a headache or some other malady. Then one Sunday, a few weeks after Emily's fourteenth birthday, she and her dad came home to an empty house. She'd always remember her father's loud gasp when he picked up the note on the kitchen table. He never let her see it, but he told her it would just be the two of them from then on.

For months Emily alternately blamed her dad and herself for her mother leaving. If only she hadn't gotten so upset when she was told she couldn't wear makeup to school or told her parents she wanted to run away. At times she thought she'd given her mother the idea.

No matter what her dad did to console her, she still felt responsible, until he finally took her to a Christian counselor, who eventually convinced her she wasn't to blame. She was being a normal teenager, but her mother wasn't equipped to deal with everyday life.

"You have a choice," the counselor had said. "Life can be difficult, but you don't have to let it keep you down. You can wallow in the past, or you can look forward to the future, knowing that your faith in Christ reserves you a place with Him for eternity." She'd paused to let Emily digest that before adding, "You have an earthly father who can only do so much, but your heavenly Father is with you for eternity—no matter what happens."

Those words had stuck in Emily's mind and gotten her through the most difficult of times. Her counselor was right. Life was extremely difficult. Fortunately, the people from church were loving, caring folks who never wavered in their commitment to help her and her father. And every summer she got to stay with Aunt Sherry and Uncle Mel and her cousins, where she felt like she was part of a happy family.

Kingston sighed again, pulling her back to the moment. She loved this dog. Maybe it wouldn't be such a bad thing for Mr. Zimmerman to move to a condo in Florida. She'd love to keep Kingston—or at least have him with Uncle Mel and Aunt Sherry so she could visit him. She just wished she wasn't so confused.

"What am I gonna do, Kingston?" she asked softly.

"Anything I can help with?"

The voice by the counter startled her. She glanced up and saw Noah standing there looking concerned.

Emily was tempted to brush him off, but what was the point? She figured she might as well be open.

"I'm frustrated about my future." She looked back at Kingston who continued staring at her with adoring eyes then turned back to Noah. "Now that I've been out of school for a while and had some time to think, going back sounds pretty good—at least sometimes—but I don't want to do it without a goal in mind."

Noah nodded but didn't say anything. He appeared to be mulling over her comment.

"I mean, I don't want to stall for time with school being my excuse. I've seen other people do that."

"Yeah, I have, too." Noah gestured to the desk. "Just remember that you always have a place here as long as you need it."

"Thank you."

"Why don't you go on home now? We've had a busy day, and Kingston and I don't want to wear you out." He smiled.

Kingston seemed to understand what Noah said. He walked over to the counter, picked up the leash in his mouth, and brought it to Emily.

"Sometimes it's hard to remember he's a dog."

Noah laughed. "I know what you mean. He's in tune to you." Suddenly his smile faded, and he looked at her as though he saw something he'd missed before.

Emily felt a familiar internal fluttering—something that had been happening more often lately when Noah looked at her that way. "I—I guess you're right. It has been a long day, and Kingston is obviously ready to go home—I mean to Uncle Mel and Aunt Sherry's."

Noah patted Kingston's head as they walked past him to the door. Emily stopped, turned to face Noah, and blinked. "I appreciate everything you're doing, Noah."

"And I feel the same about you."

Her mouth grew dry as she waved and said good-bye. Kingston looked up at her as if he wanted to acknowledge what she was thinking. For the first time in her life, she felt like she truly belonged—yet she didn't have a permanent home, a career that seemed ideal for her, or a clue about her future. What was up with that?

All the way to her aunt and uncle's, Emily chatted with Kingston. He gave her occasional understanding glances, but most of the time he focused straight ahead on the road. Their afternoon routine was basically the same, but her feelings had escalated; she felt like she might burst if something didn't happen soon. It was all up to her now.

When they pulled onto the dirt road, the dog's ears perked up. There was no doubt he knew where he was.

"We're home, Kingston."

The instant she stopped the car, Kingston pawed at the door. She hopped out of the driver's side and looked at him, which was all the encouragement he needed to hop over her seat and out the door. He ran around in circles for a few seconds, until Uncle Mel hollered that he was in the barn.

Kingston took off running toward the sound of Uncle Mel's voice. Emily went into the house to put down her handbag. Aunt Sherry greeted her as she walked into the kitchen.

"Mel has some news from town," Aunt Sherry said.

"News?" Emily lifted a carrot stick off the platter on the island and munched the edge. "What happened?"

Aunt Sherry frowned for a moment then shook her head. "I better let Mel tell you. Why don't you go on out to the barn?"

Panic rose in Emily as she followed her aunt's orders. When she got to the barn door, she paused to let her eyes adjust.

"Hey, Emily girl, come on over here. I gotta tell you something." Uncle Mel patted a bale of hay next to him. "Have a seat."

fourteen

"I talked to Dwayne this afternoon," Uncle Mel said. "Apparently there's a whole list of warrants out for Brad's arrest—some from other states."

"So what happens now?" Emily asked.

Uncle Mel shrugged. "We're not sure yet. Looks like he might be extradited, but they have a bunch of paperwork to handle first."

"What does that mean for Jillian?"

Uncle Mel offered a half smile. "Looks like Jillian won't have to worry about Brad coming after her. He'll be in jail somewhere for a very long time."

So that meant Jillian could go back to work soon. Emily had mixed feelings about that. Having Jillian back at the office would free Emily up to pursue other things—and give her time to figure out what she wanted to do with her life.

"What's wrong?" Uncle Mel asked as he paused, folded his arms, and leaned against a post. "Are you unhappy about something?"

"No." Emily slowly shook her head. "I just don't know what to do yet."

"It's tough having to make decisions," he agreed. "I remember trying to decide whether I should seek my fortune in the big city or stay on the farm where I'd always been."

"What was the turning point for you?"

He snickered. "I tried the city for about a year and quickly learned that it's not for me."

Emily couldn't imagine Uncle Mel in the city. "I could have told you that."

"If you'd been around then, I might have asked you." With

a grin, he added, "But there are some things we have to figure out for ourselves."

"So do you think I should consider farm life?"

Uncle Mel shrugged. "Everyone's different. Some people know what they want all their lives."

Emily thought for a few seconds. "Ever since I went to an art museum with my middle school class, I've wanted to work in one."

"Is that what you still want to do?"

She frowned. "I think so."

"Well, then do it. You're young, and you have your whole life ahead of you."

"Thanks, Uncle Mel."

Emily felt the warmth of his smile as he nodded. "I didn't do anything but encourage you to do what you said you wanted."

"That's exactly what I needed." She fought an unsettled feeling that kept creeping up.

"I'm glad I could help." He reached over and picked up the rake. "I better get back to work. Sherry doesn't like me being late for supper."

Aunt Sherry glanced at her as she walked in through the kitchen door. "So what do you think about what's going on?"

Emily forced a smile. "I'm just glad Jillian will be free to come back to work. I know she misses working at the clinic."

"She's a good girl but a little naive. Maybe this experience will help her become more discerning."

"I'm sure she will," Emily said. "Need some help with that?"

"Thanks but no. I'm almost done here. Why don't you go get washed up and come help me set the table?"

❧

The next couple of weeks went by quickly. Jillian had to go to court, but she didn't have to testify in front of Brad. Emily and Noah were in the courtroom to offer their support, so when Brad was led away the last time, they let out a collective sigh of relief. Emily felt a surge of protectiveness as she met Jillian's gaze.

"She's holding up quite well," Noah acknowledged. "To be honest, I wasn't sure how this would turn out."

"I was concerned, too." Emily glanced back and forth between Noah and Jillian, who stood about twenty feet away. "Why don't we go see how she feels?"

Jillian met them halfway. "I am so glad that's over with."

Emily put her arm around Jillian. "So how are you feeling now?"

"Beyond relieved." She cast a quick glance toward Noah. "And ready to go back to work, if that's all right with you."

"Of course it is," he said. "When would you like to return?"

Emily felt her insides tighten as she turned back to Jillian. Until now she hadn't really thought about how her own life would be affected by another change. Would she still be needed at the clinic? She knew she couldn't continue working part-time forever. Maybe this was the push she needed.

Jillian glanced at her, smiled, then turned back to Noah. "How about next week?"

"Perfect," Noah said. "I'm sure Emily will be glad to have you back."

❧

Noah couldn't tell what was going on with Emily, but she didn't seem herself. Outwardly she appeared happy, but he could tell there was something behind that smile. Something that he'd spotted a few times since he'd known her.

As soon as Jillian left, he gently placed his hand in the small of her back and leaned over to whisper. "Are you okay?"

She hesitated for a split second then nodded. "I'm fine."

"Wanna go somewhere and talk?"

Noah's chest constricted as she looked him in the eye and nodded. "Sure."

Since they'd driven together from the clinic, he helped her into the passenger seat then went around to his side of the truck and got in. "It's nice out. How about a park?"

"Sounds good."

Since he knew she loved roses, he drove to Ritter Park where they could sit and chat in the rose garden. She smiled as he took her hand and led her to a quiet place.

"This is so beautiful." Emily looked around at the rows and rows of flowers in various colors.

Warmth flooded him. "I thought you might like it."

After they found a place to sit, a comfortable silence fell between them. The only sound was the chirping of birds.

Finally Emily turned to him. "I'm relieved that Jillian won't have to worry about Brad anymore."

Noah nodded. "Yeah, me, too."

"That was quite a scare we had when Dwayne had to go inside and get Brad out of her house."

Noah met her gaze. "Dwayne is trying to witness to Jillian, ya know. He feels like she just needs to be surrounded by Christian love to stay strong against the evil nature of people like Brad."

Her smile added even more sparkle to the beauty surrounding them. "That's a no-brainer."

He chuckled. "As much as I don't understand it, all the things that happened with Jillian turned out to be a blessing." He paused for a moment then added, "We need to continue praying for Brad. Something terrible must have happened to him in the past."

"I'm sure." Emily cleared her throat. "So what did you want to talk about?"

Noah wasn't sure how to begin, so he figured he might as well just come out with it. He looked her in the eye and held her gaze for a few seconds before he finally said, "You."

She instantly frowned. "Me?"

He nodded. "Yes. I could tell something was bothering

you in the courtroom, and I thought you might want to talk about it."

Emily swallowed as she looked around before locking gazes with him again. "I'm really happy for Jillian, and I want her to come back to work. It's just. . ." Her voice trailed off as she seemed to gather her thoughts. "It's just that now I need to make a decision about what I need to do next."

"What you *need* to do?" he challenged.

She snickered. "Okay, what I *want* to do. I still don't know."

"You once mentioned that you wanted to become a curator in an art museum. How about that?"

"I'm not so sure I can do it."

When she looked down, he gently turned her face toward his. "Of course you can. I have a feeling that you can do almost anything you set your mind to." She'd already proven that after nearly doubling his accounts receivable deposits in the short time she'd been working for him.

"To get what I need, I'll have to go to New York."

"New York? There's a graduate art program at Marshall University."

She offered a sad smile. "Yes, but if I want to work in a bigger city, I'll need to go to NYU."

He pondered that for a moment. As much as Noah wanted to keep her in West Virginia, he cared enough to want what was best for her. "If that's what you really want, just do it. I've seen people who don't pursue their dreams, and they go through life wondering *what-if.*" As he spoke, he shuddered at the very idea of her leaving town for the big city and the possibility of not seeing her again.

Once again they fell silent. A slight breeze had picked up the scent of the roses and carried it toward them. After several minutes, Emily stood. "I'll think about it, okay?"

He nodded. "Just let me know if there's anything I can do to help you." But what he really wanted to do was tell her he loved her and beg her not to go.

Early the next morning, Emily got up and started the process of applying to NYU for their art history graduate program. Noah's words about people wondering *what-if* kept flowing through her mind. She knew her mother was one of those unhappy people, and she certainly didn't want to end up like the woman who'd abandoned the people who needed her most.

When Emily saw the cost of the program, she nearly choked. However, she'd made it through four years of college on grants and scholarships, so her next step was to find as many of those as she could.

When she had the last form filled out and in the mail, she shut her eyes and said a prayer. This wasn't easy, but nothing in her life ever had been. From the earliest she could remember, anything she wanted had been a struggle to attain. And the one thing she used to want more than anything— her mother by her side—had always been beyond her reach.

Once Jillian came back to work and got into a routine, Emily went back to part-time—mostly mornings. That gave her quite a bit of free time to help Uncle Mel or Aunt Sherry around the farm and house. It also gave them plenty of opportunities to talk and try to get her to open up. As much as she wanted to share her deepest feelings, it was impossible—and she was well aware that they knew. Each time Aunt Sherry looked at her with understanding, Emily had to turn away or risk bursting into tears. She'd learned to be strong—to not let anything get her down. At least, that was how she appeared on the outside. Inside she was a jumbled up mess.

Kingston was the perfect companion. He never left her side, and he knew when she needed a hug. Mr. Zimmerman had extended his stay in Europe, so Noah had asked if she could keep Kingston for a little while longer. Some days she hung around the clinic to help Jillian manage the paperwork, now that they had a workable billing routine in place.

"How about a raise for both of you?" Noah asked as he walked in after one of his daily deposits. "We're all in this together, so we should share the prosperity."

Noah wore a smile, but she missed seeing that old sparkle in his eye and spring in his step. Something was definitely bothering him, but she knew him well enough to know he wouldn't tell anyone what it was.

Emily shrugged. "A raise is nice, but since I probably won't be here much longer, why don't you give my share to Jillian?"

"No," Jillian said with a flick of her hand. "That's silly. If anything, you should have all of it. You're the one who got everyone paying their bills."

Noah laughed out loud. "I've never heard of employees turning down raises. Should I call the news station, or do y'all need a doctor?"

Emily grinned at Noah. "I'm just happy to be here. If it weren't for you, I don't know that I would have applied to NYU."

"You would have eventually—that is, if it's what you really want." His smile faded, and he tilted his head forward as he looked at her with an intensity that made her uncomfortable.

"Maybe so, but I still appreciate you giving me that nudge."

Jillian stood and backed out of the room, leaving Noah and Emily alone. "I'll be in the break room if you need me."

As soon as she left, Noah stepped closer to Emily. "Any idea when you'll hear something?"

Her heart pounded harder as he drew closer. "Should be any day now. I barely made the deadline for next semester."

Noah stopped, glanced down at the floor, then looked back at her, frowning. "Just let me know so I can make arrangements. You've not only gotten my clients paying, but you're responsible for bringing in more business than I can handle with one part-time employee."

"I can't take credit for any of that, Noah. Your business was growing, and I just happened to be here."

He continued gazing at her, his frown gradually softening.

"You have no idea how valuable you've been around here."

Emily sensed that his words held more than one meaning. She held his gaze for as long as she could, until she felt like flinging herself into his arms. The combination of his kindness, his love of animals, and his commitment to the Lord had warmed her heart, and she knew that if she weren't careful, she could easily fall in love with Noah.

After her experience with loving her mother who wasn't capable of loving her back, she needed to leave as soon as possible—or she'd risk another heartbreak. Emily and her father had loved her mother, and look where that got both of them. She loved her father, but he'd worked himself into an early grave to support her and help supplement the scholarships she'd gotten for college. There was no way she'd be able to endure another heartbreak this soon.

Emily was glad when Jillian returned to the desk and Noah's appointment arrived. He'd asked her to stick around for a little while, so she busied herself with finishing the paperwork she'd committed to then left for the day.

"C'mon, Kingston. Maybe we still have time to help Uncle Mel in the barn."

The dog trotted alongside Emily to her car. He knew the routine. He hopped over the driver's side and settled into the passenger's seat. All the way to the farm, Emily chatted to Kingston, who gave her an occasional glance as if to let her know he understood. When she pointed to another dog on the side of the road, he let out a "Woof!" then turned to her with a pleased expression.

As soon as she pulled onto the long driveway leading to the house, Kingston's eyes focused on the barn and his ears stood a little higher. Not only had she grown attached to Kingston, he and Uncle Mel had a special bond. She wished they didn't have to give him up when Mr. Zimmerman came home.

Kingston waited patiently as she put the car in PARK, took her handbag off the floor, and got out. The second she patted her thigh, he bounded out of the car, gave her a quick glance for approval, and as soon as he got the nod, he took off for the barn in his lopsided gallop. Emily hung back, laughed, and watched the pure joy as Uncle Mel greeted him at the door. Every day their return to the farm was basically the same, but each time, her attachment felt stronger. She was afraid that if she stuck around much longer, she'd never be able to pull herself away.

When she joined them, Uncle Mel was still smiling. "This is the nicest dog I've ever known, and I've been around quite a few dogs in my life."

"I know. Sometimes I forget he's not human."

Uncle Mel gave Kingston a final rub behind the ears before turning his attention to Emily. "So how was your day at the clinic?"

She shrugged. "The usual for me, but Noah's business is taking off. After I leave, he might have to hire someone else."

He studied her for several seconds before he nodded. "I'm sure you'll be a hard one to replace."

"Anyone can do what I do there," Emily said. "It's no big deal."

"Not according to what Noah said."

Emily wanted to change the subject—get it off Noah. "Anything I can do out here before I go in?"

Uncle Mel looked over at Kingston, who sat waiting for some interaction with the other animals. "Why don't you grab one of those baskets and get the eggs from the chickens on the east side and take them in to Sherry? We didn't finish getting them earlier."

As soon as Emily filled the basket with eggs, she waved to let Uncle Mel know she was done then headed inside. Aunt Sherry glanced over her shoulder and grinned.

"There's an envelope for you on the table by the door," Aunt Sherry said. "I think it's what you've been waiting for."

fifteen

Emily didn't waste a second. She quickly picked up the envelope with the NYU logo but paused. *What if it's a rejection?* She closed her eyes and said a prayer. When she looked at the envelope again, she forced herself to remember that if they turned her down, she hadn't lost anything.

She spotted Aunt Sherry out of the corner of her eye and let out a nervous giggle. "I might as well open it and see the verdict."

Aunt Sherry folded her arms and offered a sympathetic smile. "I can't imagine why they'd turn you down."

The second she pulled the paper out and read the first line, her heart thudded. It was an acceptance! Her mind instantly raced with all sorts of thoughts—from the thrill of having the honor of going to NYU to concern about how she'd do it. She lowered her head once again.

"Are you okay?" Aunt Sherry asked as she bridged the gap between them. "They didn't turn you down, did they?"

Emily shook her head and tried to force her voice, but her throat felt scratchy. "No, I've been accepted, but I have no idea how I can afford it."

"Did you read the entire letter?" Her aunt nodded toward the envelope still gripped in Emily's hand.

Emily took a deep breath and held it up to finish reading what the registrar had to say. "They're asking me to go there and talk to some people about money."

"Then do it." Aunt Sherry gave her a hug. "I'm so proud of you I could squeal. Imagine my niece being smart enough to go to NYU."

"A lot of people go there, but thanks, Aunt Sherry. Let me

go put this away, and I'll come help you in the kitchen."

Her aunt opened her mouth then quickly closed it. "Okay. I understand that you need some time to digest the news. Just remember that Mel and I will support you in anything you decide to do. We'll even buy your plane ticket if you need us to."

Tears stung the backs of Emily's eyes. "Thank you so much. I don't know what I'd do without you."

"So go on and do what you have to do. I'll see you in the kitchen in a few minutes."

Emily didn't waste any time putting the letter in the folder with her transcripts and other related paperwork. She took a few minutes to regroup then went to help Aunt Sherry. Fortunately they were too busy putting dinner on the table to discuss NYU.

Uncle Mel came inside just in time to say the blessing. After he finished, Aunt Sherry blurted, "Emily has some wonderful news she'd like to share."

He turned to face her with a wide grin. "I knew you didn't have a thing to worry about, Emily. So tell me when you start."

She explained that they wanted her to come up to visit before everything was final, but if everything went well in the interview, she was that much closer to getting into the master's program. "Then all I'll have to do is figure out a way to pay for it."

Uncle Mel frowned. "I thought you filled out all those forms for that."

Emily shrugged. "It might take awhile for them to come through. In the meantime—"

Uncle Mel interrupted her. "In the meantime, your aunt and I will do everything we can to make this happen for you. If the money comes through, you can pay us back. If it doesn't, then don't worry about it. We want to invest in your future."

Suddenly Emily couldn't hold back the tears. They sprang

out of her eyes before she had a chance to catch herself.

"Look what you've gone and done, Mel." Aunt Sherry stood up and came around to hug Emily. "I want you to relax about this, honey. We're just doing what a loving family does. I know you've had a difficult time of it, but there's no point in that anymore. We have more than we need, and it's an honor for us to share it with you."

Emily's bottom lip quivered as she nodded. "Th–thank you."

"Now let's eat," Uncle Mel said as he winked at Aunt Sherry. "Since we suspected that letter might be good news, your aunt made a special dessert to celebrate."

She had to fight the tears once again. Having this much support was almost more than she could handle. Even as much as her father loved her, he'd argued about her going to college, letting her know that she'd be wasting four years of having no income, and she wouldn't be able to stand on her own two feet for a long time. Guilt had overcome her when her father passed away during her freshman year, and at times she wondered if he'd still be alive if she'd taken his advice.

"When people have dreams as big as yours," Uncle Mel said, "it's just wrong for other people to get in their way. Our dream was to have this farm, and we've been blessed, thanks to the people who helped us get started."

Emily frowned. "I thought this was a family farm. Dad said you inherited it."

Uncle Mel cut his glance over to Aunt Sherry who nodded. Then he turned back to Emily. "Your dad and I inherited it together, but he wasn't interested. He sold his share to me. Not only did I have to get the money to buy him out, I had to update the barn and all the equipment."

"You paid Dad for his share? He never mentioned that."

"He most likely didn't want you to know."

Emily sat back and wondered what her dad had done with the money. It must not have been much because he'd struggled financially for as long as she could remember.

Finally she had to ask. "My parents always struggled and acted like they were flat broke. In fact, Mom used to make snide remarks about how worthless Dad was because all he knew was what he learned from being raised on a farm."

Uncle Mel's eyebrows shot up. "She said that, huh?"

Emily nodded. "I never understood that. Dad always had a job—sometimes two. I wonder what he did with the money you paid him for the farm."

Her aunt and uncle exchanged a glance, and Aunt Sherry nodded. Uncle Mel squared his jaw as he put down his fork. "He spent most of that money trying his dead-level best to keep your mother happy. When he ran out of money, she lost interest and found someone else who could buy her what she wanted."

Emily looked down at the table as she processed all that. She knew her mother constantly harangued her father about not making enough money, and she often wondered why her mother didn't go out and get a job after Emily was old enough to be home alone after school.

"I'm really sorry I had to be the one to tell you all this, but it's obvious your dad didn't want you to know what happened. Sherry and I have been talking, and since you kept blaming yourself for everything, we figured it was time for you to know the truth."

Aunt Sherry reached out for Emily's hand and squeezed it. "You've always been a good girl—the kind of child any parent should feel honored to have. We're just thankful your dad continued taking you to church. He had his flaws, but deep down, he was a good man. Some men might've caved in and denounced their faith."

Armed with all this information, Emily had quite a bit to think about. "Is it okay with y'all if I don't have my celebration dessert now?"

"Sure, honey." Aunt Sherry stood and started clearing the table. "We can do it later or even tomorrow night if that's better for you."

Emily started helping with the dishes, until Uncle Mel nudged her out of the way. "Let me take over for you here, Emily. I'd like to spend some time with my wife. Why don't you go on to your room and figure out when you can go to New York to check out that school?"

≥≥

Noah was surprised to see Emily's car in the parking lot, since he'd arrived an hour early. He pulled some of the new equipment off the back of his truck, placed it on a dolly, then rolled it to the entrance. She saw him and jumped to her feet to hold the door for him.

"Whatcha got there?" she asked.

"Some equipment that I couldn't afford until our clients started paying, thanks to you."

"Need some help setting it up?" she asked.

"I need to wait until the technician gets here." He rolled the equipment to the back then joined her in the reception area. "So why are you here so early?"

She turned away from the computer screen and looked him in the eye. "I've been accepted to NYU."

Noah froze in place as a strange feeling of dread washed over him. He was happy for her. Really, he was. Well, at least he wanted to be.

He forced a grin. "Congratulations, Emily! That's a big deal! When do you have to leave?"

Emily flashed an odd expression. "Not until next semester— but if you don't mind, I'd like to take a few days off so I can go up there for a short visit."

Noah choked back the words he wanted to say—that he needed her and didn't want her to leave—and nodded. "Yes, of course you can take off all the time you need."

Her half smile warmed his heart. "Thank you, Noah. You've been wonderful to me."

He wanted to kick himself in the backside for wishing she hadn't been accepted. Everything was running so smoothly at the clinic, and all the clients adored her. Though Jillian was sweet and did a good job, Emily added a spark to the office.

And being truthful with himself, he felt the spark all the way to his heart. At some point along the journey of getting to know her and growing his business, Noah had fallen in love with Emily. Thoughts of *ever after* had even flickered through his mind. That fact made him take a physical step back.

"Don't forget, Emily, you've helped me quite a bit around here. We'll certainly miss you." He couldn't hold back his businesslike tone.

"I know you'll probably need help training someone new, so maybe I can do that after I get back from my visit?"

He gave her a clipped nod. "That's fine." If he didn't get to work soon, he knew he risked begging her to stay. "What time is my first appointment?"

"Ten." She didn't even have to glance at the calendar.

"I'll go prep the examining room and start positioning the new equipment to make it easy for the technician to set up."

"Need help with that?" she asked.

"No." His voice was brusque, so he started over and tried for a softer approach. "No thanks."

"Okay," she said as she tucked her hair behind her ear. "Just let me know if you need me."

Oh he needed her all right—way more than he'd ever admit. Over the past few months he'd felt the change as she worked her way under his skin. The only thing he could do right now was pray—at least if he didn't want to lose his mind.

Lord, I don't know what's going on with this feeling I have for Emily, but I pray that I don't act like a jerk about her leaving. She's wonderful—everything I've always wanted in a woman. Not only does she brighten up every room she enters, she has a heart for You. She's beautiful and smart and interesting. He opened his eyes for a moment then added, *I pray for her success in anything she does. Amen.*

The morning went by more slowly than usual, in spite of the fact that Noah was as busy as ever. Emily occasionally came back to tell him something, and he made it a point to keep their contact brief. He didn't want to run the risk of saying the wrong thing—not when she was about to embark on the journey of her dreams.

But one thing kept playing in his mind. What if there was some chance that she felt the same way about him? He decided to take a chance and let her know how he felt.

"We need to talk," he said.

Emily looked at him and tilted her head. "Sure. Now?"

He hesitated then nodded. "Yes, now."

She leaned back in her chair. "Okay."

"This probably isn't the best place to do this, but I don't see that I have a choice. Emily, I've fallen in love with you."

Her eyes widened, and she opened her mouth. Nothing came out.

"I almost didn't tell you because I didn't want to confuse you. But the more I thought about it, I realized it wouldn't be fair not to let you know how I felt." He glanced down at the floor then slowly looked back at her. "Sorry if I upset you."

She shook her head. "I think I'm falling in love with you, too, Noah, but that's not enough. I don't want to risk letting go of something I might later regret."

"I understand," he replied. "I'm just glad we got this out in the open. We should always be honest with each other."

Did he dare to hope she might stay? Nah. At least not until she had a chance to check out New York.

≈

The following week, Aunt Sherry stood in the doorway as Emily zipped her suitcase. "Got everything?"

Emily nodded. "I'm pretty sure I do."

"Plane ticket, identification, toothbrush?"

"It's all here." She patted her shoulder bag. "And I have enough clothes for a week."

"Do you have the Carsons' address?"

Emily double-checked to make sure she had the slip of paper with the address of Aunt Sherry's cousin, who lived in Manhattan. "It's here."

Aunt Sherry looked at her with sad eyes. "Okay, I reckon it's time for us to take you to the airport. Ready?"

Six hours later, Emily was in the taxi on her way to Todd and Bonnie Carson's townhouse in the city. As the driver whisked her through the streets of Manhattan, she felt an overwhelming surge of fear.

What am I doing, Lord? Is this what You want for me? Or should I act on my feelings for Noah and stay in West Virginia? Please make that clear before I make a huge mistake.

"That'll be forty-five dollars." The taxi driver turned around and held out his hand.

Once she paid him and had her luggage on the sidewalk beside her, she stood in front of the building, cupped her hand over her eyes, and looked up. It sure was tall—much higher than any building in West Virginia.

She said another prayer—this time for strength—before forging ahead. Once she pushed the button to ring the Carsons' apartment, she was on her way.

Bonnie greeted her as the elevator opened. She'd met Aunt Sherry's cousin once, but she instantly felt close to her as they hugged.

"Look at you, Emily! You look wonderful!" Bonnie held her at arm's length and looked her up and down. "There's something about that West Virginia air that makes people glow. I miss it more than you can ever imagine." She took control of Emily's rolling suitcase and led the way to her apartment. "The guest room is tiny, but I fixed it up for you. There's some space in the closet, and the bathroom is right outside your door."

The building showed its age on the outside, but once they'd entered Bonnie's apartment, Emily felt as though she'd been transported into the future. Everything was so modern and sleek—quite unlike the country home of Uncle Mel and Aunt Sherry.

"This is beautiful," Emily said.

Bonnie laughed. "I guess it's okay, but it's not my taste. I prefer more traditional, but Todd likes contemporary, so we compromised. He decorated the living room, and I got everything else."

Once again Emily was amazed at the change when she got to the guest room. The walls were painted in a warm peach. The four-poster double bed, covered in a Double Wedding Ring quilt, took up most of the space in the room. There was a braided rug beside the bed, and an old-fashioned water pitcher sat on the tiny dressing table.

"Why don't you take a few minutes and put your things away?" Bonnie said as she backed out of the room. "I'm working on something in the kitchen, so when you're ready, why don't you join me?"

As soon as she was alone, Emily sat down on the edge of the bed and sighed. She'd never felt so overwhelmed in her life.

She opened her suitcase and hung up the few nice things she'd brought. Then she powdered her nose and freshened her lipstick.

When she opened her bedroom door, the smell of cinnamon overwelmed her, and she allowed her nose to lead her to the kitchen. Bonnie pointed to the baking sheet on the counter.

"Sherry said you love pastries, so I pulled out our grandmother's old recipe and baked some cinnamon buns."

Emily's heart instantly warmed. "You didn't have to do that." She took a deep whiff and grinned. "But I sure do like the way they smell. It's almost like I never left Aunt Sherry's."

Bonnie chuckled. "Have a seat, and I'll bring it to you. Coffee?"

A few minutes later, as they munched on cinnamon buns and sipped coffee, Emily almost forgot that she was in one of the largest cities in the world. It felt almost as cozy as being in Aunt Sherry's kitchen.

"What's on the agenda for your trip?" Bonnie asked. "We don't have a car, so you'll have to take the subway or taxi, but that's really the easiest way to get around."

"I can't even imagine trying to drive here," Emily said.

Bonnie laughed. "That was the first thing I gave up when I moved here."

Emily told her what all she planned to do while in the city, and Bonnie gave her some pointers about getting around to the various places. She explained the subway system in detail and even gave her a token.

"You didn't have to do that," Emily said. "I brought money."

"This will save you from having to deal with buying tickets. This is good for the rest of the week." She stood up and carried the plates to the sink then turned to face Emily. "Since you don't have anything else to do today, why don't we take a little walking tour of the area? We might even get a little shopping in while we're at it."

They spent the remainder of the day going into shops and giggling like best friends. Bonnie had the energy and youthful spirit of a woman half her age. On the way home, they stopped off at a deli and picked up some prepared food.

Todd arrived just in time for dinner. When they sat down, Bonnie reached for their hands and Todd said the blessing.

Throughout dinner, Todd talked about his ministry in the city. He was the pastor of a large congregation that had four services each Sunday, due to space limitations. At least Emily knew she'd have a church home once she moved to New York, but that didn't still the uneasy feeling about what lay ahead.

The next day, she set out for her first meeting with a few members of the university faculty. All three of them were cordial but aloof. They asked questions, and she answered them to the best of her ability. She had a list of her own questions, but she was too uncomfortable to ask any of them.

Finally, as they stood at the end of the meeting, one of the men smiled, extended a hand, and said they'd let her know very soon. "The grant you applied for should cover all your expenses for the semester—that is, if it comes through."

The woman beside him nodded. "You'll have to reapply for the next semester, but that shouldn't be a problem."

Emily blinked. "All expenses?"

"Yes," the woman said. "Including living expenses. Assuming you don't mind living in a dorm."

"No, I—I don't mind at all. I just didn't expect—"

One of the panel members stood, and the others followed suit, letting her know she was being dismissed. "You'll hear from us soon."

Emily headed back to Bonnie's place in a daze. She made her way to the tall building that offered a cozy refuge, feeling like she was in some sort of warped dream. None of it seemed real.

As soon as Bonnie saw Emily, she pulled her in for a hug. "You look like you've just seen a monster," she said. "Want to talk about it?"

"To be honest, I'm so confused," Emily explained how she'd been surprised the grant would cover all her expenses, but she still felt uneasy about everything. And worse yet, she wasn't eager to go to any art galleries. What was wrong with her?

"I can certainly understand," Bonnie said. "We'll pray about it. In the meantime, you still have a couple more meetings with faculty, so why don't you try to clear your mind until it's all over? Then we can discuss the pros and cons, if you'd like, and try to work through your concerns."

Emily was thankful for such a wonderful host. She knew that her life could possibly change in a huge way, and it was comforting to know she'd have someone she could talk to for the next couple of years.

Over the course of her meetings, people talked to her about the details of the program. They always started out stiff and formal, but when she got to meet some of the other students in the program, they all offered her a warm welcome.

Finally, when she walked out of the last meeting on the day before she was due to head back to West Virginia, she took a long look at the throng of people scurrying by. One man looked familiar from a distance, but when he drew closer, she realized she'd superimposed Noah's image over his face. That was when it hit her hard.

sixteen

This had been her dream for many years, but things had changed. She'd spent some time with her aunt and uncle, living the simple farm life that brought her a sense of peace. And she'd met Noah, a wonderful man who could be anywhere he wanted to be. He'd chosen Huntington, West Virginia, because he loved helping people and animals who truly needed his skills. And he loved her.

Now all Emily wanted was to be back in West Virginia with the people she loved, working beside Noah in his clinic and allowing their relationship to grow. Somewhere along the way her dream had changed, and that was why she felt so uneasy about being in New York. A year ago the hope of admission to NYU's graduate program and the possibility of a full grant would have made her over-the-moon happy. However, she now felt led in another direction.

In fact, the graduate art program at Marshall University in Huntington was starting to appeal to her. She'd met some of the faculty when they brought animals to the clinic, and they all seemed to be the type of people she wanted to surround herself with. Good, caring people who took pride in their campus. They didn't offer a master's in art history, but there was enough history included in their general art graduate studies that she could still accomplish her goal. That is, if her desire to pursue it ever returned. Now she was thinking she might want to stick around in the clinic awhile longer.

By the time she got back to Bonnie's apartment, she felt light on her feet. Bonnie's eyebrows shot up as soon as they made eye contact.

"You look mighty happy about something." She gestured

toward the tone-on-tone ivory and white sofa. "Let's talk."

Emily felt like she might burst with joy as she explained how she felt. "All this time I thought the only thing that could possibly make me happy was this. And now that things have changed, I feel free."

Bonnie's smile faded as she leaned forward, propped her elbows on her knees, and looked Emily in the eye. "Can you be happy working in a vet clinic, going to a smaller school, and living the simple life?"

There was no doubt in Emily's mind. "Absolutely."

"Then do it. I'm sure if you change your mind in the future, NYU will still be there." She paused for a moment before continuing. "From what I've heard, Noah's quite a guy."

"Yes." Emily looked down then met Bonnie's gaze. "He's one of the nicest men I've ever met."

"And?" Bonnie tilted her head to one side and offered a teasing grin.

Emily's cheeks flamed. "He and I finally admitted our feelings for each other. I'm falling in love with him, and I'd like to see how things can be between us."

Bonnie leaned back and belted out a hearty laugh. "That's obvious. Now why don't you go on back to West Virginia and let him know how you feel?"

"I have to admit it scares me."

"Don't live in fear, Emily. I know you've had some tough times, but you can't let that hold you back from what you really want. Noah's a good guy. I suspect he has some fears as well. Sherry told me that you and Noah are perfect for each other."

"What if she's mistaken?"

Bonnie shrugged. "Then at least you'll know. Life's too short to hold back on matters of the heart. You need to trust God with your feelings and pray for His guidance. I bet He brought Noah into your life for a purpose. In fact, I'm sure He did. From my perspective, it all looks like God's work—from your decision to stay with Sherry and Mel while you figured things out to coming here and realizing it's not what you really want."

"It's just that Noah's such a wonderful man. He never gave up on his other assistant, even though her boyfriend talked her into letting him into the clinic after hours. I think his kindness and gentle understanding make this even more difficult, since he's like that with everyone."

"Listen to me, Emily," Bonnie said with uncharacteristic firmness. "He's a kind man who loves the Lord. He takes care of animals and people in need. Don't you think he's also capable of having a loving relationship with a woman?"

Emily chewed her bottom lip and thought about all that Bonnie had said. It certainly made sense. Finally she stood up. "I need to go pack now. I guess I should call my faculty advisor and let her know I've decided to decline their offer—at least for now."

"Why don't you sleep on it tonight and call in the morning? I don't want you to have any regrets."

The next morning, Emily awoke feeling better than she'd felt in months. As soon as she had a cup of coffee, she called NYU and turned down the offer. Now all she had to do was go back to West Virginia and talk to Noah. Hopefully he hadn't started looking for someone to replace her. She knew Aunt Sherry and Uncle Mel wouldn't mind her sticking around a little bit longer until she had everything in place.

Bonnie went down to hail her a cab and gave her a hug before she got in. "I'll call Sherry and give her your flight number."

"Thanks for everything," Emily said. "I don't know what I would have done without you and Todd."

"You would have done just fine, but I'm glad I got to share this experience with you." She leaned over after Emily got into the cab. "E-mail me and let me know how it goes."

All the way back, Emily mentally rehearsed how she'd ask Noah if she could keep her job. She'd explain that she loved West Virginia and discovered how much she enjoyed working with animals. Hopefully he hadn't changed his mind and decided he was better off without her.

Her plane landed ten minutes ahead of schedule, so she took her time walking to the baggage claim area. When she rounded the corner, she had to blink to make sure she wasn't seeing things. What was Noah doing here?

"Hi there," he said as he walked toward her with a purpose. "How was the big city?"

Emily's lips quivered as she tried to act nonchalant. This wasn't the time to have that talk with him. "Good. Where are my aunt and uncle?"

He tilted his head and made a hurt puppy face. "You don't want to see me?"

"Oh no, it's not that. I just thought—they are okay, aren't they?"

"Yes, they're fine. I just volunteered to pick you up. You don't mind, do you?"

She grinned at him. "I'm glad you're here."

"I was worried there for a moment." He gestured toward the conveyor belt that had started moving. "Let's get your stuff and get out of here. We need to talk."

Emily thought her bag would never arrive. She was eager to leave the airport and find out what Noah wanted to talk about. What if he wanted her to leave sooner than they'd originally planned? What if he'd found the perfect person who wanted to start right away? All those thoughts filled her mind, until she thought she might pop with worry.

He tossed her bag into the back of the truck and opened her door for her before running around to his side. The second he got in, she knew she couldn't hold back anymore.

"Noah, I realize this makes me sound like a flake who can't make up her mind, but I really don't want to move to New York and go to NYU and work in a museum, and I love animals, and—"

He laughed. "Whoa, Emily, slow down. Let's start from the beginning. What happened?"

She closed her eyes and took a deep breath. *Lord, please help me get this out without scaring Noah*. When she opened her eyes and turned to face him, she saw the grin on his lips.

"What's so funny?" she asked.

Noah reached for her hand. "You. I know what happened in New York. Sherry's cousin called her and said you've decided not to take their offer."

Emily nodded. "It's a really good offer. Very generous. But it's not what I really want."

As they pulled up to a red light, he turned to her. "What do you really want, Emily?"

She swallowed hard. "My job?"

The light turned green, so he accelerated and focused his attention on the road. "Okay, you have that. I'll never find anyone else who can do the kind of work you do with such a heart for animals."

"Thank you."

He cut a quick glance back at her. "Is there anything else you want?"

Her breath caught in her throat. "Like what do you mean?"

Noah shrugged. "I don't know. You seem awfully nervous about something, so I thought there might be more."

Emily didn't dare tell him what else she wanted because if he knew it was him, surely that would scare him away. But she didn't want to lie either.

He patted her hand. "You don't have to tell me now. We can talk when we get to Mel and Sherry's place."

Kingston didn't waste any time running out to the truck to greet them. The instant Aunt Sherry opened the screen door, he darted out and stood waiting by the truck.

"Hey, boy," she said as she got out of the truck and patted his head. He leaned into her side and let out a deep sigh of joy.

Aunt Sherry and Uncle Mel stood on the porch and

waited. Noah brought Emily's bag inside and set it down.

He turned to Emily. "Why don't you go on in and change into some jeans? I'd like to go for a walk if you're up to it."

"Sure," Emily replied. "It'll be good to stretch my legs after being on the plane. Be right back."

Uncle Mel carried the bag to Emily's room then went back out to chat with Noah. Aunt Sherry followed Emily inside.

"We have a special dinner for your homecoming," her aunt said.

Emily laughed. "All your dinners are special." She patted her midsection. "And delicious."

"I'm just tickled pink you're back." She hugged Emily and gently pushed her into the room. "Now change out of your traveling clothes and go for that walk with Noah. You don't want to keep him waiting too much longer."

Emily gave her aunt a curious look, but Aunt Sherry just grinned and pointed to the room. "Okay, I'll hurry."

When Emily finished changing, she took off outside to find Noah sitting by himself on the porch steps. He stood and reached for her hand.

"Let's go down there," he said, pointing toward a clump of trees on the opposite side of the house from the barn. "I'd like a little privacy."

"Okay." Emily didn't understand his need for privacy, but she trusted him. "Looks like y'all got some more rain while I was gone."

"Yeah, we did, and I didn't get much sleep because of it. Some of the farmers can't handle much more rain after the last flood. It was an exhausting experience that'll take time to recover from."

"Was everyone okay?" She looked at him.

He stopped, turned her around to face him, and shook his head. "Not really."

"Did you have to move the livestock again?"

"No, not that. No one got flooded this time, but that wasn't what you asked."

Emily tilted her head. "Huh?"

"You asked if everyone was okay, and I said not really. I wasn't okay."

Fear gripped Emily. "Jillian?"

He shook his head. "No, not Jillian."

She was puzzled. "What's wrong?"

Noah held on to both of her hands and took a step back, never breaking their gaze. "I think I've been hit hard by love."

"What?" Her voice cracked.

He looked down at the ground before looking back into her eyes. "Emily Kimball, I'm in love with you. I didn't realize it until you started talking about going to NYU. I didn't want to lose you. And I don't mean as an employee."

"Why didn't you say something?"

"I wasn't sure about things."

He shook his head. "I knew you weren't, which was why I didn't want to push too hard. I didn't want to stand between you and your dreams."

"I appreciate that," she said. She couldn't stop herself from smiling. "You're such a kind, selfless man."

"You think so?"

"Yeah, I know so."

"When Sherry told me you were coming back to stay, I was beside myself." Noah pulled her close until she could feel his heart beating. "I wanted to talk you out of going, but I held back. I didn't want to scare you."

"Oh, I'm scared," she said. "Very, very scared."

He groaned. "I was afraid of that."

"But only because I love you, too."

Noah suddenly froze. "You said that before, but I wasn't sure you meant it." He tilted her head. "Are you sure?"

"Uh-huh. Very much. In fact, the whole time I was in

New York, all I could think about was how miserable I'd be without you."

"Emily, I am now the happiest man in West Virginia. No, make that the whole USA."

She laughed. "Let's see how things go, now that we've admitted our feelings. This is all new to me."

After he walked Emily back to her aunt and uncle's house, Noah had to leave. One of the farmers had called his cell phone and said he had a cow in labor, and it looked like she might need some help.

"I'll see you first thing in the morning," Noah said as he turned and ran toward his truck. "I hope this really happened and it's not a dream."

Emily smiled and waved as Noah drove away. She had the same fear as Noah, that it might be a dream.

૨૦

Noah wanted to shout his feelings at the top of his lungs, but he needed to contain his emotions—at least until he finished delivering the calf. He arrived at the farm in the nick of time.

"I think it's breech," the farmer said.

Noah got down to business and managed to save the calf with the farmer's help. When he stood up and shook the man's hand, he got a big grin and slap on the back.

"So when's the big day?"

Noah turned his head slightly and narrowed his eyes. "What big day?"

"I hear you and Mel's niece are sweet on each other. I figured you were about to get hitched."

"Where did you hear that?" Noah asked, unable to keep the grin from sliding over his lips.

"Little birdie told me."

"I'll have to have a talk with that little birdie. Getting hitched sounds pretty good to me, but in the meantime, try to keep it to yourself. I haven't asked her yet."

"You sly dog. Just make sure you send me an invite."

ada

Emily got to the office early the next morning and turned on the computer. Everything she'd taken for granted before seemed fresh and new to her now. She loved everything about this place—from the curve of the counter to the bell on the door. With Kingston by her side, she felt like she could conquer the world.

To her delight, Noah arrived fifteen minutes later. "Hey, I thought you might be here. Got a minute?"

"Sure," she said. "What's up?"

Noah crooked his finger and motioned for her to go outside with him. He locked the door and led her toward the back, through the cluster of trees, and to a clearing, where he stopped and turned her to face him.

"It's come to my attention that people are talking about us," he began.

She opened her mouth, but he gently put his finger over her lips. He didn't look unhappy, so she tried to erase the fear that welled in her chest.

"I'm not saying I mind them talking, but I do think they need something concrete to talk about." He pulled something out of his pocket and got down on one knee. "I know we just admitted our feelings for each other yesterday, but I'm a man who knows what he wants, and I go after it."

Emily giggled. This was such a strange experience for her that she had no idea what to do. So she just stood there and stared at him.

He kissed the back of her hand then studied it for a moment before he opened the box. "Will you marry me, Emily?"

Her knees grew weak when she saw the beautiful pear-shaped diamond ring. When she tried to answer, her mouth was so dry nothing would come out. So she nodded.

"I sure hope it fits. Your aunt said she thought this was your size." He pulled the ring from the box and slipped it on her finger.

"My aunt?" Her voice came out in a sudden squeak. "She knew about this?"

He rubbed his neck. "Um—yeah. I sort of needed to talk to her so I could get you a ring you'd like. I'm not very good at picking out jewelry."

Emily splayed her hand and looked at the dazzling ring. It was perfect—exactly what she would have picked for herself.

"Well, do you like it?"

She threw her arms around his neck and squeezed him as tight as she could. "I love it!"

Noah had to peel her arms away to give her a kiss. Afterward, he looked into her eyes and stroked her cheek. "If you always act like this when I give you jewelry, we better go out and buy the biggest jewelry box we can find, because I'm gonna do it a bunch."

Emily laughed. "It's not the ring, silly. It's you."

"Well, in that case, come here, Emily, and let me kiss you again."

epilogue

"Hold still, Kingston." Jillian grabbed the Great Dane by the collar as Uncle Mel fastened the wedding rings to the attached pillow. Mr. Zimmerman had decided to go ahead with his plans to move to Florida, and Emily happily agreed to keep Kingston.

As soon as Mel had the rings secured, Jillian straightened up and turned to Emily. "Ready?"

Emily turned to Uncle Mel, who winked. "Ready as I'll ever be."

Jillian gave the signal to the church organist, who turned and started playing. Emily's heart lurched, so she lowered her head and said a prayer of thanks. She opened her eyes in time to watch her maid of honor, Jillian, and Noah's best man, Dwayne, guide Kingston toward his position as the ring bearer.

As Emily's heart stilled and her nerves steadied, Uncle Mel gave her hand a squeeze. "We're up next," he whispered. "You're a beautiful bride, Emily. Noah's a blessed man."

Emily felt her cheeks flame—not with embarrassment but with joy. "I'm the one who's blessed."

Her uncle laughed and nodded. "Let's agree that you're both blessed and get this show on the road. You don't want to keep your groom waiting."

All heads turned the instant the music tempo quickened, and Emily felt a flood of emotion as her entire life changed. For the first time ever, she had no doubt what she wanted—and that was to be the wife of a man whose faith in the Lord was as strong as hers.

After they said their vows, Noah lowered his head to kiss Emily. Suddenly she felt something nudging between her and her new husband. When she looked down, she saw Kingston straining against the leash, with Jillian on the other end, wearing an apologetic grin. He was attached to his family, and he obviously didn't want to be left out. Everyone laughed as Emily and Noah included Kingston in a hug. They finally turned to walk up the aisle as a family—husband, wife, and family dog.

A Letter To Our Readers

Dear Reader:
In order that we might better contribute to your reading enjoyment, we would appreciate your taking a few minutes to respond to the following questions. We welcome your comments and read each form and letter we receive. When completed, please return to the following:

Fiction Editor
Heartsong Presents
PO Box 719
Uhrichsville, Ohio 44683

1. Did you enjoy reading *Noah's Ark* by Debby Mayne?
   ❑ Very much! I would like to see more books by this author!
   ❑ Moderately. I would have enjoyed it more if

   _____

   _____

   _____

2. Are you a member of **Heartsong Presents**? ❑ Yes ❑ No
   If no, where did you purchase this book? _____

   _____

3. How would you rate, on a scale from 1 (poor) to 5 (superior), the cover design? _____

4. On a scale from 1 (poor) to 10 (superior), please rate the following elements.

   ____ Heroine   ____ Plot
   ____ Hero   ____ Inspirational theme
   ____ Setting   ____ Secondary characters

5. These characters were special because? _____

_____

_____

6. How has this book inspired your life? _____

_____

_____

7. What settings would you like to see covered in future
   Heartsong Presents books? _____

_____

_____

8. What are some inspirational themes you would like to see
   treated in future books? _____

_____

_____

9. Would you be interested in reading other **Heartsong
   Presents** titles? ❏ Yes ❏ No

10. Please check your age range:

    ❏ Under 18   ❏ 18-24

    ❏ 25-34   ❏ 35-45

    ❏ 46-55   ❏ Over 55

Name _____

Occupation _____

Address _____

City, State, Zip_____

E-mail _____

PAINTED DESERT

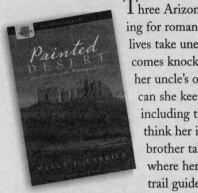

Three Arizona women are not looking for romance, but as their modern lives take unexpected turns, love comes knocking. Blaire has inherited her uncle's ostrich ranch, but how can she keep it when everyone, including the handsome manager, think her incompetent? Jazmyn's brother takes her on a hiking trip where her path crosses a secretive trail guide. Can Jazmyn and Thor work together to clear the past? Maddy agrees to help her friend's brother on a nature photo assignment, but will burns from past loves keep these two forever apart? Can love pain a new day of promise for each woman?

Please send me ____ copies of *Painted Desert*. I am enclosing $7.97 for each.
(Please add $4.00 to cover postage and handling per order. OH add 7% tax.
If outside the U.S. please call 740-922-7280 for shipping charges.)

Name_____

Address _____

City, State, Zip _____

To place a credit card order, call 1-740-922-7280.
Send to: Heartsong Presents Readers' Service, PO Box 721, Uhrichsville, OH 44683

Presents

Great Inspirational Romance at a Great Price!

Heartsong Presents books are inspirational romances in contemporary and historical settings, designed to give you an enjoyable, spirit-lifting reading experience. You can choose wonderfully written titles from some of today's best authors like Wanda E. Brunstetter, Mary Connealy, Susan Page Davis, Cathy Marie Hake, Joyce Livingston, and many others.

When ordering quantities less than twelve, above titles are $2.97 each.
Not all titles may be available at time of order.

SEND TO: **Heartsong Presents** Readers' Service
P.O. Box 721, Uhrichsville, Ohio 44683
Please send me the items checked above. I am enclosing $ _____
(please add $4.00 to cover postage per order. OH add 7% tax. WA add 8.5%). Send check or money order, no cash or C.O.D.s, please.
To place a credit card order, call 1-740-922-7280.

NAME _____

ADDRESS _____

CITY/STATE _____ ZIP_____

HP 11-09